I0633110

# We Are Made of Stars

a novel by

## Jameson Currier

Chelsea Station Editions

New York

*We Are Made of Stars* by Jameson Currier
Copyright © 2024 by Jameson Currier.

All rights reserved.

This book, or parts thereof, may not be reproduced in any form, without the permission of the publisher.

*We Are Made of Stars* by Jameson Currier is a work of fiction. Any references to historical events, real people, or real places are used fictitiously. Names, characters, places, and events are the product of the author's imagination or are used fictitiously. Any resemblance to actual events, places or persons, living or dead, is entirely coincidental.

Cover art by Jameson Currier
Book design by Peachboy Distillery & Designs

Published by Chelsea Station Editions
New York, NY
www.chelseastationeditions.com

Paperback: Print ISBN: 978-1-937627-33-1
Ebook ISBN: 978-1-937627-75-1
Library of Congress Control Number: 2024917209

First Edition

# We Are Made of Stars

After a decade of mistakes, a struggling writer leaves Manhattan to start over in a small college town. Populated with egotists and narcissists, Jameson Currier's resilient and unflinching *We Are Made of Stars*, a "memoir in the form of a novel pretending to be a memoir," reveals a gay man's journey through grief during the early years of the AIDS epidemic.

## Praise for the writings of Jameson Currier

"Currier is adept at drawing a fine line between the erotic and the tragic, and at telling stories that 'although personal, are also the stories of our community.'"
—*The New York Times Book Review*

"A writer who consistently surprises and delights, Currier's dynamism will surely carry his literary career to higher heights."
—*Bay Area Reporter*

"The breadth of Currier's personal experience is evident in his writing, which is moving without resorting to melodrama, familiar without feeling clichéd."
—*Windy City Times*

"As a writer, Currier should be lauded for his creative decision to avoid the all-too-common formulaic trappings of most current novels written for and about gay men."
—*Lambda Literary*

"Jameson Currier's kind of fiction can recreate reality more accurately than a cinema verité account of our daily lives."
—*The Washington Post Book World*

Also by Jameson Currier

A Gathering Storm

Based on a True Story

Dancing on the Moon: Short Stories about AIDS

Desire, Lust, Passion, Sex

Paul's Cat

Still Dancing: New and Selected Stories

The Candlelight Ghost

The Forever Marathon

The Haunted Heart and Other Tales

The Man That Got Away

The Third Buddha

The Wolf at the Door

Until My Heart Stops

What Comes Around

Where the Rainbow Ends

Why Didn't Someone Warn You
About Prince Charming?

# We Are Made of Stars

"The final mystery is oneself. When one has weighed the sun in the balance, and measured the steps of the moon, and mapped out the seven heavens star by star, there still remains oneself. Who can calculate the orbit of his own soul?"
—Oscar Wilde

"We are all made of stars."
—Jameson Currier

This story is not about Maggie, beautiful brown-eyed Maggie with her thick, hippie curls, tank tops, and patchwork skirts, a coworker I met after I moved out of Manhattan, though she is an integral part to this tale and provides me with a place to start. It was 1989, a year when we were both in our early thirties when Maggie and I worked together as assistants for a famous architect in a notable college town. Our desks were on the top floor of a renovated Colonial-style house, a windowless space under one of the eaves in a spot that would normally be the apex of the attic. Maggie and I sat on stools at the opposite ends of a shelf carved into the shape of a boomerang that was meant to be a tabletop workspace. In the warmer months and the months when warmth was required, heat collected around our oddly-shaped tabletop because the slope of the roof and the walls of our workspace trapped it from fleeing elsewhere. The office equipment around us—computers, fax machines, electric typewriters, photocopiers, office phones, and desk lamps—offered us additional warmth, or, in the summer months, superfluous heat. Some afternoons in the summer the temperature at our workspace might soar close to three digits. I would tell Maggie that I thought it was ironic that a famous brand-name architect known for his innovative exteriors of neoclassical architecture could save and renovate a historic jewel of small-town America such as the building where we were working, but he didn't know how to design the interior as a functioning office space where people could do their jobs sitting at desks without passing out from heatstroke. All that was needed in our workspace was a window, or since there wasn't a vertical wall to anchor such a basic amenity, a skylight or vent that popped open—or at least the equivalent of a fist shoved through the roof—to allow the accumulated heat to escape. How hard could that be for an architect who had convinced billionaire business moguls that he could design elaborate multimillion-dollar convention halls, hotels, and auditoriums?

Maggie, stripped down to a tank top and a thin, cotton skirt, would stare at me with her large brown eyes full of fury and disgust and leave her desk to go into the tiny bathroom that we were lucky enough to have next to our workspace, probably because of a building code requirement or as an afterthought to seal off the indoor plumbing at the top of the house. She would turn on the cold-water faucet, fill up the sink, and dunk her head into the water, wetting her long curls until they were soaked black. The bathroom, rarely cleaned or attended to, would never have any towels, so she would return to her desk, a trail of water puddling around her swivel stool. She would sit motionless as if she were meditating or silently planning revenge. I would calmly mention that I didn't think it was safe for her to work soaking wet in front of the electrical equipment on our desks and the wiring that covered the floors around our feet. What if she were electrocuted? I was hardly prepared to save her and risk my own electrocution. "This is nothing," she would say, twisting the strands of her hair so that water would trickle onto the front of her tank top, and stare at me as if I was mad.

Of course, I was mad. When I wasn't sweating and flushing myself with water from the nearby sink just as she was, I was trying not to admit that I had made a terrible mistake, or, rather, a series of terrible mistakes. It wasn't the excessive heat or the horrendous working conditions that made me crazy. I was confused and shaken. Something had unnaturally changed in my life.

I'd taken the position as an office assistant because I thought it would be low-pressure and little responsibility. My assignments were to wait and type and mail packages and help where needed. I dressed comfortably and professionally— in a button-down cotton shirt and chino pants that by day's end would be heavy and stiff from repeatedly sweating and drying. Maggie was not my antagonist, nor was she a mirror held up to reflect my unhappiness. She was her own story. She was fretting about her marriage. She had only been married a few months—five to be exact at the time I begin to tell this story—and her husband, Bryan, was an illustrator—a graphic designer for magazines—so he worked at home and took day trips to New York or Philadelphia or Baltimore to present his designs, often staying overnight—and a constant source of concern for Maggie since the responsibilities of raising his teenage son fell on her, not Bryan. But Maggie was also open about her full extent of marital troubles. She would pout her lips before speaking. "I thought I was marrying security," she told me. "And not just money-wise. I can't trust myself, so how can I trust him?"

Maggie made me realize that everyone was confused about sex and relationships and it provided a common thread for us to develop a friendship. Luke, Bryan's son by his first marriage, was a high school sophomore and Maggie had found herself unexpectedly answering questions from her stepson about school topics such as civilization, psychology, politics, and biology because Luke was an avid reader. Maggie had decided that she liked spending time with the son more than she did with his father because the son was sensitive, inquisitive, and intelligent. "He asks me questions," she would tell me. "He cares about what I think and why. We have conversations about important things. I feel like I'm young and still learning."

Maggie had come to expect deep, thoughtful conversations with everyone. She felt it was important for us to talk about a variety of subjects so that we could get to the heart and truth of our opinions and how we had formed them. I wasn't a talkative guy. I kept my secrets to myself and my emotions bottled up. I felt I struggled with everything: how to prevent a check from bouncing, how to keep my car running, how to get the sweat stains out of my clothes. So our conversations were often one-sided; when Maggie wasn't pursing her lips and shaking her hair over the failures of her husband or seeking better answers to her stepson's questions, she was talking about what she really wanted to do with her life, or what she had hoped to do before she landed in a shared office space with our scalps pressed to a ceiling.

Maggie was a classically trained pianist, the daughter of teachers who had raised her in this college town; her mother taught English and American History at a prep school; her father was a professor whose course, A Survey of the British Novel, was a popular choice for college freshmen. Maggie's concert career never took off, and she had landed in the San Francisco Bay Area after splitting from a bisexual yoga instructor, so she had taken gigs as a keyboardist with a variety of pop and rock bands, and for a time turned into a rocker chick who had affairs with drummers and lead guitarists, until a series of quakes sent her back to the East Coast. Maggie was grateful to leave California and the hippie-rock concert life behind. "Too much time pretending to practice," she said. "And way too many drugs." Maggie felt she was too sharp-witted to be a post-hippie rocker chick. Now she wrote poems about being abused, sober, and clean. Abused as a girlfriend, a stepmother, a daughter, a musician, a wife, a patient, and an office assistant. Sober from booze. Clean from brushes with cocaine and heroin and prescription pills. She called her poems "tremors," and she was convinced that she had invented a new form of poetic expression and because of this she now had an identity and self-worth separate from her abusers and addictions. Sometimes she would tilt her head and tense her lips and read aloud a stanza of one of her newly composed poems and ask my opinion. Something like:

*a daring adjective*
*shapeless alone*
*as adroit conjunction*
*blazes wounded fact.*

The earnestness of her dramatic delivery and analytic poetry always made me laugh—not just because of the exaggerated poetic approach to self-examination but of my fear that she was speaking the truth. "You're channeling Sylvia Plath a little too closely," I told her after hearing one particular brutal recitation about our warmish workspace that included the breathless examination of a "sincere inferno."

"Really?" she answered. "My birthday falls on the same date she died."

"I hope that's just a coincidence."

"She was a great force."

"Who met a tragic end."

"Don't you believe in the stars?"

Maggie held my eyes steadily, as if she were reading my mind, and I felt both vulnerable and relieved to be the focus of attention, hoping someone might save me or at least wake me up from my own nightmare.

"You mean like astrology? And psychics?"

She nodded and drops of water from her hair dampened the desktop. "I used to date a guy who lived on Haight Street who wanted to do my astrology chart because he thought I might share some of her psychic turmoil, but we always ended up doing...other things."

My eyes widened with both alarm and glee at the idea that I might be sharing an oven-warm box with a psychic Sylvia Plath twin.

"I should find out what happened to him," she continued. "Last I heard, he was in Baltimore. We should have our charts done."

Then she asked, "What's your sign?"

"Libra."

I felt her smirk, her calculation, and her wicked and brilliant mind flexing with syntax. Maggie was an Aquarian; creativity and chance were here ruling planets. We worked at our desks in silence until she began to read to me from her journal.

*Cheer to my gloom,*
*Gloom to my cheer,*

*Yin and yang*
*Are not so different.*

*Our time together*
*Necessary and endless.*

*We are not so different*
*You and I.*

*We are made of stars.*
*Unique and alike.*

*We are light and dark*
*And dark and light.*

*Dust and tears*
*And dirt and fears.*

*We are yin and yang and*
*Yang and yin.*

*Comets in different directions*
*To the same destination.*

The brand-name architect was one of a group of five world-famous designers who embraced modernism, though the employment agency representative who had sent me to his firm told me he had shifted to postmodernism. I didn't exactly understand either reference. I always thought of the interior of his office building where I worked as a well-planned joke: walls built in front of windows and doors to prevent them from opening, stairways that led to nowhere, and a labyrinth of halls clogged by three-dimensional scale models of building projects and trophy cases full of citations, commendations, and photographs. None of it made any sense to me; it looked like a haphazard mess. Nothing functioned as it was supposed to function.

I didn't work directly with the famous architect, but for a team of wannabe-famous ones who were drafting the interior and exterior specifications for two big-scale projects that were under construction: a corporate office building of a legendary film company located in Hollywood and a convention hotel at a notable resort destination in Florida. The managing architect of this team had been a surfer in his prior life, or so I had imagined his past. Greg was tall, thin, and lithe, deeply tanned with shaggy dirty-blond locks. I wasn't remarkably attractive; I benefitted from a boyish appearance and height and failed to possess a noticeable sexuality that could provoke or disturb either sex. I never formally or officially "came out" as gay to anyone at the firm, though I had reached the point in my life where I did not have anything to hide about my past. On my first day, I noticed several employees I suspected might be gay, including the office manager. Maggie, however, sensed my history within seconds of meeting me. "Well, shit," she said when we first shook hands, "I bet you've been through as much crap as I have."

Greg was quietly suspicious the day that I first showed up to be his assistant, but after I had typed up his label and memo and left it on the side of his desk before he had a chance to change it any further, we had reached an uneasy alliance. The uneasiness wasn't because he could overhear my phone conversations about symptoms and doctor appointments and protests and phone trees with my friend Jesse back in Manhattan while I was waiting for other labels and memos to type, but from the fact that when Greg appeared with work for me to do, he was forced to crouch and lean over my shoulder because of the slope of the roof above our workspace, and in doing so he would balance himself as if he had shown up to whisper a secret in my ear. It was a daring pose if you didn't understand the circumstances—if I moved my face even a millimeter, our lips would touch. He did this instead of calling me on the phone or buzzing me on the intercom and asking me to come to his desk in another part of the building.

"That dude is sending you some serious vibes," Maggie remarked one afternoon after Greg had lingered at my desk changing words as he wrote and rewrote a memo, shifting himself as close around me as possible.

Greg was about four years older than I was, which would put him in his mid-to-late thirties, married, the father of two kids, a boy and a girl, both just starting school—kindergarten and first grade—so I always thought of him as a careless pretty boy who had been reluctant to leave the surfboard behind in the garage and become an adult with responsibilities. And I did admire him for this transformation. Some days he would come to work with wet hair, and I would imagine him shirtless, emerging from the foam of an ocean wave. Some days I would take messages from his wife, Colleen, and walk down the short flight of stairs to the large, spacious room where he worked with his team of sub-architects and drafters. I was always amused by the view from Greg's desk of the employee parking lot behind the building—another example of the glamourless aftereffect of the design of an industry baron who had abandoned function for artistic features. I would leave the phone messages in a bin at the side of Greg's desk, knowing that he would show up at mine later, inquisitive, leaning over me to ask more details of where his wife was, what tone of voice did she use, and did she want a call back?

Greg's wife also worked for the brand-name architect. Colleen had once been the architect's assistant and was now helping with interior design projects, picking out paint colors and matching fabric swatches. She had blonde highlights, a flirtatious attitude, and a slow Southern drawl which I detested, because it reminded me of the girls I had avoided in high school, and I always detected a smirk in the tone of her voice, as if I had been the subject of bedtime talk with her husband. Her desk was in another wing of the renovated house where we worked and impossible to reach unless you took three different flights of stairs. She never paid her husband—or his assistant—a visit, which was why I think Greg so freely hovered over me whenever he had the chance.

"What would you do if you were me?" I asked Maggie one day. "And you had a handsome surfer guy leaning over your shoulder asking you about his wife?" I was flushed from the heat and the lingering scents of Greg's deodorant, toothpaste, and shampoo.

She shook her hair, pulled in her cheeks, and burst into an evil cackle. "I'd take him into that bathroom and fuck his brains out."

I smiled and reached for a tissue to dry the sweat that was dripping into my eyes. I had no desire to pursue Greg. He was a wet dream and someone I could easily fall for, but I felt no positive energy from him. When I looked at him, my gaydar went blank. Which is why I felt that he was only baiting me. And I would be the one with the black eye and out of a job if one of us took a misstep.

"Tommy Gunn has lost his ass," Jesse's voice laughed in my ear when I answered my work phone one morning. Jesse was calling from his office desk overlooking Union Square in Manhattan. His nasal voice was a tone of whisper, gossip, and concern. "Remember those shorts he wore in the parade?"

Jesse was a second-tier editor of a mathematical journal. Like many writers, he needed a day job to support his habit of writing metafiction and ambush journalism about his life as a gay man with HIV. He always lost his sense of humor when I asked him if he fact-checked the equations.

"Skin tight," I replied. I was alone at my workspace at the boomerang desk in the attic and turned off the small fan at the side of my desk so I could hear Jesse better. "So tight you could see his circumcision scar."

"If that's where you were looking," Jesse answered. Tommy Gunn had been a popular gay adult porn star and a particular obsession of Jesse's. Jesse had seen Tommy the evening before at the ACT UP meeting at the community center in the West Village. ACT UP was a group of activists, mostly gay men and lesbians, "united in anger and committed to direct action to end the AIDS crisis." In a short space of time, they had become infamous for protests and demonstrations, disruptions to the status quo of Wall Street and Congress and the pharmaceutical industry, insurance companies, and the media. They wanted lower drug prices and quicker clinical trials for new drugs and more news coverage and safe-sex campaigns and needle-exchange programs and an expanding agenda of social changes around HIV and AIDS. Jesse was in an affinity group that seemed to have no affinity within or without the organization. When he wasn't gossiping or complaining about lesbian misrule and the group's obsession with the Catholic Church, he was ready to march and protest and practice civil disobedience to push his own agenda—himself.

Jesse was short and narcissistic—large-nosed and big-chested with skinny legs and nicely defined biceps, and often sporting a dark, badly groomed mustache. He was unafraid to shed his clothes or his feelings, but only if you listened to his stinging critiques of anything on his mind or within his sight. He was loud and defensive even before he learned of his HIV-positive status. Jesse identified as a gonzo-journalist and metafiction writer, but his accusatory and abrasive wisecracking caused a lot of resentment and created a spectrum of detractors, precisely his ambition. He talked and wrote only about himself, his failures at love and sex, until, that is, he uncovered his own declining health. He was never ashamed of sharing the dirty details of his health issues and side effects from prescriptions and treatments. His anal warts, acyclovir side effects, rectal fissures, and diarrhea were public topics in the letters and articles he published in any of the gay newspapers, porn magazines, and bar rags that would print them and he had turned his writing—as many others had—into a battle cry. But his observations—and his cynicism and sarcasm—never failed to make me laugh. And cringe.

"You can see for yourself," Jesse added. "I invited him to my beach party on Saturday."

"You mean your beachless party."

"They'll be sand and water and plenty of hot guys. And Tommy Gunn."

Jesse lived in a fifth-floor walk-up in Hell's Kitchen. He had painted the walls of his apartment lavender and taped up pictures of handsome, beautiful guys he had ripped from underwear ads, gym promotions, and porn magazines, introducing his wall collage of shirtless men and nude physiques to guests as "my perfect boyfriend." Even if he could afford a share in a Fire Island Pines summer house, it wasn't his scene. His annual beach party was his friends showing up to his apartment in their bathing suits, drinking and hanging out on his fire escape. It was always an event where it was possible to arrange more than one hookup. I liked Jesse's parties because they were something to do that didn't cost me money. I had lots of bills and expenses that seemed to follow and haunt me whenever I forgot about them.

"You can meet Jeff and tell me if he's going to dump me." Jesse said.

"Jeff?"

"My new boyfriend."

"When did this happen?"

"I met him on a phone line a couple of days ago."

"Is he cute?"

"I'll find out Saturday if he shows up. You can help me decide."

Even though we spoke several times a week, Jesse and New York seemed far away and an event from my past, as if I were watching a helium-blown party balloon disappearing into the sky. Jesse represented a reckless part of myself I was ready to shed—the young man who had thought that being good at sex was his path to love. "Jesse…"

"Frank's funeral was yesterday," he said. "I thought you would have the decency to be there."

I felt both guilt and grief. Frank was a librarian in the Village. He was a bearish man of dark hair and muscle—I had met him at one of Jesse's parties, only to learn later he was in an open relationship with "a man I could never walk out on." But he was an avid reader and a devoted theatergoer who was always willing to share his likes and dislikes with me. Jesse was doing his best to provoke me. The last three months I had lived in the city, I had attended a wave of funerals and memorials and I refused to summon up an image of them to remember Frank.

"I can't afford to come back to the city," I said, hoping my answer held not only my financial constraints, but also my emotional ones.

Jesse took the opportunity to practice his own brand of tough love. "What are you doing?" he asked me.

"I'm waiting for something to type." Out of the corner of my sight, I saw Maggie return to her stool and our shared workspace.

"No, I mean what are you doing there? You should be here. In the city. Down the block. Ready to meet me on 46th Street and march and then go out for brunch."

"Jesse, that's you. That's your life."

"I thought you moved out of the city to write."

"I did. I will."

"You should write about Frank. And the guy who gave me herpes, and the one who gave me crabs and that time with the threesome in Provincetown where I got the clap."

"I can't tell everyone's story."

"So, tell your own."

"I'm trying to change who I am," I answered and knew the moment that I said it that it was a mistake and a misstatement. For all my insistence on how I wanted to be a writer and I needed to find a story and the space and freedom and clarity of mind to write, I hadn't expressed myself clearly.

"People don't change," he said with anger. "You'll always be selfish." Then, he hung up on me.

His criticism stung with a bitter aftermath because for once I felt I was doing something for myself. I walked into the bathroom and splashed my face with water.

Back at my desk Maggie was scribbling in her journal. I knew she was poised and ready to talk. I turned to her and said, "Tell me a secret. Tell me something I shouldn't know about you."

"I've had two abortions," she answered.

"I can't do your chart without it," my friend Wade explained to me.

This was years before, in Wade's apartment in Chelsea. I was in my early twenties; Wade was a few years older. He seemed an unlikely candidate to be interested in horoscopes and astrology. Wade was a dark enigma to me: a chiseled jawline, brooding black eyes, and a bad boy reputation. His apartment was decorated with cast-off furniture and wood crates from corner markets, and embellished with books and piles of clothing, paper plates with crumbs and stains, and empty bottles of beer. His closet was full of leather jackets, chaps, and flannel shirts. One crate was filled with dildos of various sizes and colors.

Wade was the first friend I made after I moved to Manhattan. I met him when we worked together at an answering service on Seventh Avenue. I had seen the job ad in an entertainment trade weekly tabloid that listed auditions for stage roles. I started a job taking messages my third day in the city. Wade had been brought to the city from a small town in Pennsylvania by an older male photographer to be part of a fashion ad campaign, but the photographer cast him aside when he discovered Wade was sleeping with the other models—both guys and girls. We both worked various shifts at the answering service and often sat side by side, trading comments about the strung-out clients and our hungover coworkers. Wade knew all the dirt—who was sleeping around, who sold drugs, who haunted the backrooms and the baths. Wade was getting back on his feet, working on his survival strategy that didn't involve "so many drugs." He liked to pretend he was my protective older brother. I had a deep crush on him, the way someone might have on a Hollywood star, but I knew he had no sexual interest in me when I learned that he had already had sex with two of our more attractive coworkers: one, a dancer with a shaved scalp and large thighs who accused Wade of giving him an STD; the other, a muscled clone with a bushy mustache who had hooked up with Wade in the "meat rack," the area of sandy dunes and bushes between the two gay resort communities on Fire Island.

I kept in touch with Wade after we both moved on to other jobs. I often asked him to go to a movie or a play when I was offered free tickets from an agent or publicist, knowing he would refuse to join me because he would find the experience boring and pretentious, but it would take me to the top of his mental "to do" list and he would call me up on another day at the last minute and ask if I wanted to go with him somewhere. I would meet Wade at his apartment, where he would offer up a smoke or a tote. I was enthralled by his outrageous behavior; he was surprised by my naïveté. I wanted to experience his kind of adventures, though he would wave his big paw of a hand and say, "that's not for you" and talk me out of experimenting with anything other than a "fingerprint of coke" before we headed out together to a bar or a club.

Wade once offered to draw out my natal chart, something he did on the side for "clients," though what sort of "clients" were never detailed to me, but his casual remarks about enemas, "golden showers," and "cuff marks" gave me a clearer idea. The chart was contingent on knowing the time of my birth, something my mother could not easily pinpoint, other than supplying in a breathy sigh, "It was early in the morning, darling. You were a premie. We didn't expect you to survive. I was trying to forget as much as I could so I wouldn't remember any unhappiness."

"Too bad," Wade said, when I relayed the news that the time I was born was also not indicated on my birth certificate. "You've got the same birthdate as Oscar Wilde. It would be cool to see the comparisons of the charts."

I was surprised that Wade knew the date of Oscar Wilde's birth, or even aware of the existence and history of Oscar Wilde and which, at the time, I don't think I fully knew or understood myself. Wade explained that when he was learning how to create natal and astrology charts, he studied the charts of celebrities and public figures that were printed in textbooks and could be found in libraries. "Of course, I was trying to find if there were sex lines and patterns, so I went right to all the known degenerates," he explained. Wade was an Aquarian; he was born on the same birthdate as James Dean. "You can find his chart in any good library," Wade said. "I studied it for years, trying to figure out how I will crash and burn."

One Saturday, Wade called and asked me to go with him to a bar on the Upper West Side. I lived in a small apartment in the West Village and the thought of trekking uptown on a Saturday night seemed silly when there were so many opportunities downtown. But I went with Wade because I was always hoping that he would look around the bar and be dissatisfied that there was no one he would want to have sex with and then realize that it was time to give me a "try." Before we left Wade's apartment that evening, I noticed a small red bump on the side of his chin and when I asked him about it, he said he had nicked himself shaving.

I took Wade's answer as the truth—I had never had a reason to question it, unlike the way my friend Mitch lied about his illness. I should clarify that this is not a story about AIDS, but being a young, sexually active gay man during the early years of the epidemic in New York City cannot be removed from this story. It's hard to depict the fear and uncertainty and anger and sorrow it unleashed. I've often played the "what if" game about those I've lost because of the disease. It, too, is as senseless as infusing a chart of the stars as a guide of what might happen in your life. Nothing, nothing, will bring a person back from death. Nothing in the stars can change that. That's why this is a story about grief and how it can reshape and recast the person you are and the person you want to become into something else, without ever loosening its nasty grip.

My dislike of Mitch was not immediate, though he was loud and opinionated from the time I met him during my first weeks in Manhattan—and not long after I met Wade. Whereas Wade could pretend to be stoic and calm, Mitch loved to be the center of attention, the elitist in the room, telling you about something you hadn't seen and why you would hate it or remarking about someone's voice or mannerism and why he found it comic and annoying. Mitch's purpose was to make you feel small and unimportant, questioning your motives and even your existence. He was a critic-at-large for an entertainment trade daily, writing pithy reviews of recent movies and theater performances, adding scathing digs "to keep everyone honest." He loved announcing himself as "New York's youngest critic." It was an open secret that he had gotten the job because of his father's wealth and investment in the daily paper that Mitch wrote for, so the thing Mitch coveted most, and seldom achieved, was earning someone's respect.

I spent many afternoons and evenings sitting across the table from him in dimly lit bars and restaurants that I couldn't afford, trying to convince myself that Mitch might be physically attractive or emotionally sincere and realizing he was neither one. Mitch's career objective was to win a Tony or an Oscar or any award that could bring him more notoriety and fame to accompany his wealth, but he wanted someone else to do his work for him. I once ran into Mitch's editor at a bar in the West Village, who confessed before the first sip of his drink that Mitch's articles and reviews required a lot of editing and rewriting by his fellow staff members, right down to the invention of his "scathing digs." Many people disliked Mitch and I tried to be as objective as I could be, at times trying to believe that Mitch's persona had been one he had invented, when it hadn't—it was who he was. Mitch fell into a habit of phoning me daily, detailing his reviews and conversations and attempts at luring some overly attractive and unavailable man into sex. I was a good listener and usually available to listen to Mitch. Mitch's vices were the bathhouses and sex clubs, but he found more success with escorts he could hire hourly to show up to a hotel room.

I also think Mitch got off on how inexperienced and unworldly I was, still so optimistic and aspiring even after failing and being quickly beaten down by the demands of the city, and he loved to burst my hopeful balloon with his devilish, or maybe even evil, streak. "There will always be someone younger and more handsome," he told me one night when we went together to a party and we had both failed to be noticed by a man we found attractive. "Don't confuse sex with love," he said to me one morning on the phone when I described to him my feeling about another man who had just left my apartment. And once, when I was bemoaning a man who had said he didn't want to see me again, Mitch said bluntly, "If you want to get over him, go out and get laid. That'll knock him right out of your brain."

I walked away from Mitch many times, mostly because I couldn't keep up financially with him— Mitch wanted to go to the newest, trendiest, hottest scene, which usually translated into the most expensive restaurant or bar or hotel or club or performance space in the city. I couldn't afford these places and I was never easy with Mitch picking up the tab. I always felt the chit would come due. I also felt Mitch never saw me. He had no interest in anything in my life—I only served as a witness to his adventures—a reflection less judgmental than a mirror. Mitch didn't show an iota of interest when I said that I wanted to be a writer, because Mitch felt it had nothing to do with himself. This is not a story about Mitch, but an admission that Mitch's over the top personality kept me curious because it so over scaled my own and I tried to break away from him, I really did. He was another mistake in my life but he was also someone I thought I might be able to write about—the unbelievable truth that fiction cannot invent, but perhaps I could be a writer who conquered this, like Fitzgerald's Nick Carraway documenting Jay Gatsby.

Mitch was a decision I made as well. I remember the night he confessed to me the results of his HIV test—he'd been going on for two weeks of worry and he was the first person I knew who tested positive. He was angry and in denial—an emotion I hadn't witnessed in him before. He swore me to secrecy; he swore me not to tell anyone about the therapist he began seeing, or the acupuncture therapy he was going to try, or the consultation he had arranged with a clinic in Geneva.

Somehow Mitch convinced me to care about him. Or I convinced myself. One evening, a few months after he had tested positive and had announced that he was "scaling down" the number of his reviews he was writing, he was to meet me outside a movie theater in midtown—we were going to a screening together—and he never showed up. I paced back and forth on the sidewalk, trying to convince myself that he had given me the wrong theater, the wrong address, or the wrong date, or the wrong time, walking to the corner to call his apartment from a phone booth, running out of change and going to the deli to buy something to get more change, to walk back to the phone booth and call his apartment again, only to hear his answering machine click on, and then running back to the theater to check to see if I had missed him showing up. I imagined him dead, passed out from too many drugs. Hours later, sometime in the early morning when he responded to my messages on his answering machine, he said that we had never made plans to attend the screening. It was a deliberate lie. It took me several more phone calls before he broke down and said that he was in the emergency room that night. That was the moment that I decided I would try to take care of Mitch. Another mistake I made.

Mitch once told me if I stopped smoking, I would be a perfect husband. He said this the rainy evening I brought him home from the hospital and I went to sit on his fire escape to light up a cigarette before I made him his dinner. His comment made me feel sad because it highlighted one of my many flaws. A few days later, as I was wiping away his missed attempt to reach the toilet, he lifted his head from his bed, widened his eyes at the sight of me cleaning up his mess, and said he loved me and never wanted me to leave him. I tried to accept this as a compliment, but I recognized his gratitude as self-serving.

I mention these details and stories of Wade and Mitch because in hindsight I had made a choice. One day I got a call from Wade asking me to come to his apartment for a party. It was more than a week away and by the time the day of his party arrived I had forgotten about it. I had forgotten about it because I was taking care of Mitch— rushing to the stores after I finished work to pick up his medications and groceries and bandages and ointments. A week went by and then another week and then another, and then Mitch was in the hospital and next I was trying to get him settled back into his apartment. Then I received a phone call from Wade's sister. The moment she introduced herself I understood what her news would be. Wade was gone.

I was devastated. As I grappled with grief, I wondered if forgetting and missing Wade's party was a deliberate choice, that I subconsciously knew it was impossible for me to give Wade the sort of attention that I was giving Mitch. I did not have the mental or physical space for both. In my grief it became another "what if" game. "Game," of course, is a wrong choice of words. And "mistake" or "regret" only make the memory bitter.

The first story I ever wrote was about a boy who turned himself into a postage stamp and mailed himself to another galaxy. I was nine years old and an avid reader of science fiction and fantasy novels. Years later, I could interpret that story as wanting to escape my life, but I didn't have a miserable or tortured childhood that I wanted to flee. I was a studious boy who wanted adventures.

I might have been a fantasy writer if I had not discovered the theater. My first role was a walk-on in a high school production of *Guys and Dolls*. I saw myself as an indistinct teenager, but in the production, I was suddenly a cool guy singing and dancing. On stage, I could become someone other than myself, better looking or more charismatic, and because of the applause—and friendship with other performers—I thought I wanted a career in the theater. I chased the idea of being an actor, then chased the dream of being a director, then thought I could be a playwright. But I wasn't good at writing on-stage dramatics.

After college, I moved to Manhattan, still chasing the desire to work in the theater until I realized I wanted to be a writer, but the allure of the theater never left me. I began writing a series of comic tales about a group of traveling musical actors, based on adventures I had had with college friends. These stories allowed me to write easily about gay and lesbian characters and their relationships and desires because the characters were based on my friends and myself. I never thought of my stories as a realistic slice of life or my characters being outsiders or part of a subculture or counterculture or an expression of the times. My sole purpose was to entertain, make a reader laugh at the absurdities of chance. I wrote of missing props, pratfalls, slapsticks, revenge recipes, mistaken identities, and bizarre obsessions.

I wrote during subway rides, on my temp jobs, on scraps of paper, napkins, and stolen pieces of stationery, sometimes memorizing phrases in my head until I could find a time to write them down. I wrote in longhand on notepads, in cursive or printing, and sometimes a hybrid of both. I typed on a manual typewriter in my apartment until I could borrow time to retype on an electric one. I never talked to someone about my writing. I rarely let anyone read my work—I wrote to make myself happy and entertain myself. I was too proud of the passion I felt for a story to have someone easily dismiss it and create a doubt within me that I should abandon this desire.

I finished a manuscript of comic, episodic stories that read as a novel and photocopied it at a temporary job when no one was monitoring me. I mailed it to several publishers in the city, hoping editors who had previously published any sort of fiction about gay men might have an interest in my stories. It was politely rejected and, as I searched for more editors to read the manuscript, I also searched for ways to make it better.

The first writing workshop I joined was not a good fit. It was sponsored by an Upper West Side writing school where the writers were more interested in being destructive than constructive. No one wanted to read a story with a gay character. One writer claimed that if my main character had been straight, there would be no reason to tell the story. Another workshop was only beneficial because the moderator, a college writing professor, passed out a reading list he gave to his college students. It was like receiving a free education.

But the more I learned about the craft of writing the weaker my desire was to continue; I thought I was doing everything wrong. I considered myself a failure. And I lost confidence in my lighthearted adventures. Life was also becoming more uneasy; I felt I was avoiding a truth about expressing my concerns. Things were changing in an alarming way: confusing news reports of a contagious illness among gay men. A gay cancer? A gay pneumonia? A gay plague? I'd always believed that I had never made a choice to be gay—that it was inherently part of who I was biologically and mentally and why I felt no shame over being gay. But the idea that there might be a disease that targeted gay men rattled me.

The news continued, shifting and revising. Next, there was the discovery of a retrovirus. Backlashes and discriminations and op-eds of fears and rebuttals. I saw this as a changing moment. I didn't want adventures in backrooms and baths clubs; I wanted to find a boyfriend and navigate the changes together. Instead, I became worried and anxious. I stopped feeling able to make plans for my life. Wade found "workarounds." Mitch was angry over any "public health closure," but he went to a doctor over any worry. I was working in a publicity office when a gay coworker called in sick and never returned to the job because he was in the hospital with a strange set of symptoms. I began to be suspicious of my own health, over-examining a leg rash or a stomach ache or an eye twitch. I wrote lists of sexual partners and our sexual acts, and then a list of my symptoms and aches and worry spots, then I began attempting essays about my growing confusions. Time passed. More things changed. I listened and read. I could no longer write without thinking I was avoiding what I needed to understand.

And then I heard of my college friend Jack. It wasn't that we were estranged, or no longer friends—he'd been the trick of a fraternity brother and we always traveled in different circles. Jack hadn't moved to Manhattan to be an actor or performer—he worked as a broker for a Wall Street trading firm. He lived in an expensive apartment on the Upper East Side. I'd seen him once at a bar and another time at an alumni party. I heard a rumor about his death before I realized it was Jack who had died—a stockbroker committing suicide by leaping off his apartment's balcony when he learned he had AIDS.

Months later, I wrote a story about a gay man who commits suicide and its impact on his family and friends. My research included news articles, obituary notices, alumni newsletters, hometown church bulletins, conversations with friends, interviews with a hotline volunteer, and my own fears. Putting the story down on paper, organizing a timeline and ideas and words gave me a sense of accomplishment and a temporary release from anxieties.

I joined another writing workshop. But they did not want to discuss the story. A fortyish woman who lived in Brooklyn and I knew to be a lesbian asked to table the story for another meeting. I didn't return to the workshop. Months later, I saw a postcard pinned to a bulletin board at a bookshop in the Village about a gay men's writing group looking for new members. I called the number and a wisecracking guy with a nasal voice asked me personal questions about my favorite sex acts and past tricks. It was Jesse.

I mentioned to Jesse that I was beginning to write stories with darker and more personal themes and that I was looking for feedback and criticisms and discussion on my structure and characters and style of writing. I offered to mail him a story and if he wanted me to join the group, I would be glad to participate.

There was a pause on the other end of the phone, as if it had been rehearsed.

"Good," he said. "I always love a good cry."

Any daily horoscope column points out the contradictory nature of those born under the sign of Libra—shy but self-assertive; affectionate yet solitary; reserved but obsessive—though I think my most inherent trait is that of being a good listener— hoping the storyteller—whether he or she be a friend, a playwright, a stand-up comic, a singer, or a novelist—can deflect my focus from myself for a few minutes. But it was never easy. Mitch said I was a worrier. He gave it to me as a compliment late in our friendship. "It must be an intrusion to you," he added. "But it's a comfort to others."

Maggie had become a new worry spot for me. I thought of her as too vulnerable to others and my overcompensation was the desire to be protective of her. I worried that any small thing could tip her into some sort of addictive behavior. I occasionally scanned her exposed arms and wrists to see if I could tell if she was using needles. I judged her to see if she was hungover or was drinking on the job. She didn't struggle with her job, but I didn't think she was equipped to handle the people she worked with and I began to take more note of her behavior. She always seemed on the verge of tears, and I found her the type of woman who sought out sympathy with hugs and reassurances, the kind which could be turned into a plea for deeper feelings. Maggie worked with a team of architects and draftsmen who sat in another large room on a floor below our workspace. They were a humorless bunch, the managing architect a pompous man with a shock of white hair and a bigger shock of a stomach who would send one of the draftsmen, usually a college intern, up to our perch with work for Maggie to type and mail out, possibly because the pompous overweight architect felt too cramped in the space where we worked. Maggie's beauty was too large to be contained in our small shared space, so her visitors would stand over her, ogle her breasts, and smile like fools. Maggie expected anyone who showed up at her desk to make a minimal effort at a conversation before giving her any work to do, so I was always witness to awkward banter about TV shows or pop songs that generally made me explode into giggles and bury my head against my desk. Maggie was also unorganized and never had paper or staples or shipping labels or tubes or boxes at her side of our work station, so she would swivel around on her stool and ask if she could borrow something she would never replace, usually tapping me on the elbow, apologizing for interrupting my personal space.

I don't know what it says about my character that I can attract and befriend narcissist after narcissist. Maggie, like Jesse and Mitch, was someone I could never give enough attention to satisfy their ego. I knew I was a growing disappointment to her. She was someone who couldn't do something alone and many times I was reluctant to take the role of being her companion or compatriot. I would stand beside her when she took cigarette breaks beside the front door entrance, watching her drag and exhale, nodding as she suggested things to do after work together, to come over for dinner when Bryan was away, or to walk with her to see Luke's softball team playing in the park. I found it best to have my own agenda—an excuse to go the library, hear a lecture, or plans to see a play at the college theater—I had to devise my own agenda to avoid being swept into hers.

But it was impossible to avoid her outside the office. It was a small college town with only a main shopping street unless you drove to the strip malls of stores along the highway a few miles away. I ran into her several times—with her husband Bryan, or her stepson Luke, and a couple of times with her mother, a frowning, thickset woman who looked at me as if I were a naughty student. It made me nervous to stop and chat with Maggie when she was with her stepson; he was an attractive boy—black hair, long eyelashes, and wisps of a beard that would soon need regular shaving. I was concerned about being out and gay to someone young and impressionable who might be questioning his own identity. This was something both Mitch and Jesse disliked about me, my willingness to blend in instead of provoking curiosity.

One Saturday, I ran into Maggie on Main Street. I had biked through the college campus and was walking my bike back to the cottage I was renting at the edge of town. This wasn't long after our conversation about astrology charts and poetry vibes and Maggie was alone, out on a quest to know more about "crystals and shit" because she thought they "were infused with metaphors."

"I need all the good vibes I can muster," she said. "Healing energies. Chakra rejuvenation."

Maggie believed in all things cosmic: zodiac signs, lucky talismans, essential oils, and bewitching fragrances. I followed Maggie down a side alleyway and locked my bike against a stairwell. There was a "new age" bookstore on the second floor she wanted to check out.

Inside, the store smelled of incense and candlewax. There were carousels of cards and self-help books, and counters of crystals and stones and silver jewelry. Maggie drew the long curls of her hair into a bun and secured it with a clasp, pouted her lips and tilted her head, and confided in the store clerk, a thin woman with frizzy hair wearing a Renaissance-fair inspired outfit. "I need to save my marriage," she said. "I want to have a baby."

I was surprised by the statement—Maggie had not clued me in on this new strategy, perhaps because I might have mentioned the rigors of motherhood to her and suggested she stop smoking. I walked away from the two women to a bookshelf and studied the titles on the spines. I thought of myself as a bundle of spiritual and psychological negativity, of neither help or consequence, and there was a time, not too long before, that I would have searched out alternative herbal therapies and self-love meditations and healing stones. I noticed that there were no titles on HIV therapies or dealing with grief. Another clerk, a woman who seemed disinterested but suspicious of me, as if I were a male presence threatening her female "safe space," asked if I was looking for anything in particular. I indicated I was with Maggie, then asked if the store had any cassette tapes to help quit smoking. She directed me to a counter and frowned as I looked at the recordings. I didn't have the extra income to splurge on a tape of affirmations accompanied by Celtic guitar, and I wandered over to a bulletin board where business cards were posted for readings and massages. I saw that Maggie had made her way to the cash register and was purchasing a bag of crystals. She held them in her hand for me to observe and I stood to the side and nodded, not reaching out to touch them. I thought it was a foolish purchase—a cry for help no one would hear—but I kept my cynicism quiet.

"These should help," the Renaissance dressed lady told Maggie. "But come back if you need something stronger."

Maggie mentioned to the sales clerk that we worked in the large white house at the edge of town, but had been reluctant to drop in to the store.

"Stop by whenever we're open," the clerk said. "You're always welcome to come here for advice."

Then she looked at me, as if she had read my palms. "You, however—You're just an observer. I can tell you are only passing through."


I left Manhattan after Mitch's death, after closing-up his apartment, sorting out his estate with his lawyer, and scattering his ashes in Central Park with his mother and sister on a cold, rainy afternoon. I was burned out and deep in debt. I had agreed to help move some of Mitch's furniture to his aunt's house in Philadelphia; Mitch's cousin had rented the van and we drove to a suburban house, where I left the cousin and several antiques. On the drive back to Manhattan, I had stopped to eat at a deli in the college town. On the bulletin board was a postcard for the rental of a small "gatekeeper's cottage." I called the realtor from a pay phone on the street, found her office a few blocks away, and drove the rental van to look at the cottage. It was a small stone house beside the gates of a large estate. The owner of the estate no longer used this gated entrance—a grander driveway had been constructed several years ago. The owner was looking for someone "other than a student" to rent the cottage; a property manager would take care of yardwork, maintenance, and billing. The cottage had been built in the 1920s. There were three large rooms with vaulted beam ceilings, a small kitchen and bathroom. The doors had inset stained glass windows with an art deco design. But the selling point was that the monthly rent was less than my West Village apartment.

There were times during Mitch's illness that I dreamed of being elsewhere—one, was to attend a graduate school where I might earn a Master of Fine Arts in Creative Writing, thinking that I might someday cash it in as a teacher after I had finished publishing all the novels I was destined to write. I filled out questionnaires for a half-dozen writing schools located outside of New York City, took the required exams, and obtained my college records, and budgeted expenses so that the application checks would not bounce. My writing sample was a polished version of the story of the impact of a gay man's suicide. I hoped and waited for good news and in the process, I realized this was one more step in distancing myself from a future in New York. I was ready to leave. But there was no good news. Mitch died. And the graduate schools sent me rejection letters.

I never thought I might be too old to go back to school. I refused to believe that I could not learn more and teach myself everything that a graduate school writing program might hope to do. I had already decided that I would leave New York, so I rented the gatekeeper's cottage.

I thought I could sit down and write about the things that had happened to me in New York City if I could step away and look back objectively at my past. But my first few weeks in the college town were filled by the novelty of being out of the city and the release of responsibility over Mitch's health— the previous tenant had left behind a bicycle, and I biked to the nearby parks and hiked their paths, awed by the simple and natural presence of trees and grass and dirt and rocks. I'd lived in Manhattan for a decade from the age of twenty-two to thirty-two. I worked as a bartender, a proofreader, a messenger, a dog sitter, a waiter, a librarian, a publicist, and a jewelry salesman in a large department store in midtown. I thought of my life in the city as simply going from one building to the next, one place to the next. The last two years I had been caring for Mitch while I worked temporary office jobs, my mind filled with noise and questions. I learned a lot while I lived in New York. I learned about wanting it and making it and having it and getting it and not getting it. I also learned that talent isn't often given to the young and willing. On those long, solitary bike rides in the country, I realized I needed to heal myself, to keep learning, and to make some changes—to stop smoking, to stop drinking to escape my unhappiness, to find a discipline to write, to find a path to self-respect, and to find a means to support myself. And somehow on this path, I hoped I might fall in love.

In the evenings, I stood outside the stone cottage, staring at the magnificent portfolio of stars that could never be seen in Manhattan, until I grew tired and restless and retreated inside to watch a video I had rented from a store in town. I soon realized, of course, that I couldn't write very fast and needed a job to pay rent, buy gas, and put food in my mouth so I could take more bike rides and continue to stare at the stars. Most of all, I was lonely and ready to meet someone. I thought everything would be easier away from New York—not just finding a job and starting a career—but meeting someone, finding romance or companionship or a relationship or just someone special who would stick around and be supportive.

There was a weekly newspaper that printed personal ads of gay men seeking others—some for quick sex, others for long-term relationships. The newspaper was a free weekly, available in a rack beside the door at the video store on the main street outside campus. I read the pages of personal ads regularly, composed replies to guys my age who enjoyed reading and theater and the movies, and enclosed my photograph in the envelopes, hoping as I biked to the post office that my response was crafted smartly enough to find the right guy, even if my photograph failed to interest someone. I felt I was just an ordinary guy looking for the right person.

I was surprised by the responses. Some guys only wanted to talk on the phone. Others were anxious to meet. I met a chain-smoking editor, a bald bodybuilder, several men who had just broken up with boyfriends, and a number of guys who were already in a relationship, but looking for "something better." Sex was easy to come by with any of them if that was what I wanted, though I didn't find that sort of hit-and-run completely satisfying.

This story is a memoir in the form of a novel pretending to be a memoir, so I am reluctant to reveal my sexual history and details except in the broadest terms. I had sex with guys before I arrived in New York; I had sex in college, I had sex in New York before the epidemic, I had unsafe sex after safe sex guidelines had been suggested. I had sex in my bed, in others' beds, in closets and bathrooms and backrooms and bathhouses. This may be interpreted that I was hedonistic and easy and just interested in sex. But I always thought sex might lead to something else, something emotionally deeper and more serious.

I kept my dating adventures private. I didn't want encouragement from Maggie or criticisms from Jesse. I'd been through a number of dating adventures in Manhattan: phone lines, personal ads, even a matchmaking service where I struggled to describe my ideal man. My ideal man didn't exist—I fell in love a thousand times a day—walking to work, riding the subway, at intermission at the theater, in a doctor's waiting room. I didn't want to write down that I wanted a tall man with a beard when the right guy for me might not be tall and prefer not to have a beard. What I wanted was someone who wanted to be with me. Mitch thought I was too particular. Wade thought I wasn't specific enough. I was a victim of my own low self-esteem. I always worried that I would be a disappointment as a boyfriend because I struggled so much with money.

One evening after helping my elderly neighbor—Rick, a farmer who lived with his wife Sarah in a small house beside the northern field of the large estate—he didn't own a car and needed someone to drive him and his wife to the hospital near the highway to see a doctor—I realized that I was waiting to be chosen by someone and, perhaps, that was the wrong approach, that I might have more luck if I was part of the selection process.

To change my direction once again, I took out my own personal ad to find a boyfriend. There was a word limit tied to the cost of taking out the ad: I listed my particulars: *GWM, 5'8", 140 lbs., brown hair, green eyes.* And then I added: *"nice guy, nice mind seeking same."*

I was overwhelmed by the volume of mail that arrived at my post office box in the college town—notes and letters and photographs from other heartbroken, forlorn, and lonely gay men. I disliked having to read the responses and judge them into yes, no, and maybe piles. I found it difficult to reach out and contact someone. I worried this would be a new pile of mistakes, that I was purposely overlooking the person I was seeking. I would hardly describe any of this as an educational or worthwhile experience, though I tried to be open-minded with the responses. After dinner, sitting on the couch in the cottage, I would spend hours talking on the phone to get to know a guy, someone who seemed to have everything in common with me, but then we would meet and I would know instantly it was not going to work because I didn't find him attractive—physically or otherwise. As anticipated as it was, blind date after blind date, it also became an addictive blur—the hope that the next responder would be a better fit than the one who had just been dismissed.

Yes, I had sex with some of these guys too, but the experience was full of frustrations. I didn't want a sexual desire to define me. I wanted to be in love, but it all seemed to start with sex. It was like being back in Manhattan looking desperately around a bar, except everything was being played out at a slower speed.

Maggie disliked the attic job at the architectural firm as much as I did; she liked the stability of a regular job but was always open to considering other options for employment and income. She returned several times to the new age bookstore and befriended its Renaissance dressing owner, Angelica. On the side of her workspace there were now books and pamphlets on interpreting the Tarot. She had worked out an exchange deal with Angelica: Maggie would teach piano to Angelica's eight-year-old daughter, Claire, in exchange for "spiritual and interpretive lessons" from Angelica, on learning how to do a Tarot reading.

"In a year I could be giving readings at the store," Maggie told me. "Angelica says I have to learn to speak more about a customer—or a client—than myself."

"Does that mean you have abandoned your poetry?" I asked.

"It's all symbiotic," she answered. "The more I understand others the more I will understand myself."

"Is that what Angelica told you?"

"She didn't have to."

I knew Maggie wanted to read my cards before she asked. "I don't think that's a good idea," I answered after she made her request. "I'd rather know more about you."

I suggested I listen to her give a reading of her own cards.

"Angelica said reading cards is like dreaming," Maggie explained as she shuffled her newly purchased deck. "You enter a space where there are other spirits and try to understand what they are telling you. You ask the cards a question, and sometimes you get an answer and sometimes you get an answer to another question. What question do I ask them?"

"That's not my question to give you," I said. "Then you would be answering my question and reading my card. What question do *you* want to ask them?"

"Fascinating," she said and smiled. "This is so complex." After a beat, she asked, "What do we do?"

She shuffled her deck of cards again. She withdrew a card from the top. It was the Eight of Pentacles. She looked at the card, and pulled a pamphlet from the side of her desk and spent a quiet moment flipping through the entries, finding one, and reading its summary. I took the opportunity to turn the fan speed down lower so I could better hear her voice, then realized it was a mistake, because it made our workspace warmer.

"This card means work," she said.

"And how do you interpret it?"

"It's what we are doing now. Or what we want to do. Refining a skill. Practicing a craft."

"Like you are doing now. Practicing reading a Tarot card."

"Or what you are doing. Or want to do. Such as writing. I asked a question with a collective subject. '*We.*'"

"What we both want," I added. "Being persistent at another skill? To keep working at it? Or doing good work? Work that is meaningful?"

"Are those your questions?"

"I asked them collectively."

"My question was directed to life elsewhere. Outside. Away from these jobs. The work that we are doing that is meaningful to us. The small things that matter, the details that build and shape our worlds. We're persistent to this other work outside of here because we love it, or if we don't love it, we love what we're working toward. The hard thing isn't that we work, it's that we don't abandon it."

She shuffled and asked, "What do we do?"

She pulled another card from the deck. It was the Three of Swords. She pulled the pamphlet off her lap, looked at the index, then silently read a passage.

Then, she read aloud: "The Three of Swords represents rejection, sadness, loneliness, heartbreak, betrayal, separation, and grief."

I wanted to laugh, but my astonishment overwhelmed me. "Sometimes it matters which way the card is placed on the table," I said, trying not to own the reading of the card. "Whether it is pointing toward the questioner or the interpreter. Or which way you pulled the card."

Maggie looked at the card, looked at her book, and lifted her eyes to meet mine.

"We should stop here," she said. "I promised Ian I would get his package out today."


There was an emptiness some mornings, as if a part of my body had been amputated but I could still feel where the limb was attached. I tried to feel something in its place, but the pain was elsewhere, coursing through my veins as if it were an icy blood. I didn't know how to move. I didn't know *why* I should move. The noise in my mind was silent until I realized it was silent and then it filled with anger and disappointment and disbelief and denial. I hated Mitch. I hated his attitude and opinions and how his body failed him. I hated the walk to his apartment, the extra keys I had to carry, the stops I had to make to bring him the current issue of a magazine or the candy he wanted. I hated the lists of groceries that I had to buy him, the phone calls I had to make to get an IV stand delivered to his apartment or the IV bags I had to keep chilled in his refrigerator. I hated that there was no one else to take charge of his life. I hated greeting his family and friends as they visited and took time away from him that I had wanted to share. At the last moments of his life, he became everything of my own.

The moment I arrived at the cottage in the college town I realized that I had these vast amounts of time to fill that in Manhattan I could ordinarily overcome by an overwhelming list of errands or by simply walking through the streets, from neighborhood to neighborhood to neighborhood, visually and mentally and physically challenged until I was exhausted and could return to my apartment. In this new life, I tried to ease grief through routines. I would exercise, shave, shower, clean the cottage, and then think I had overcome the resurrection of any memories and walk out to my car, unlock the door, slip the key into the ignition, and hear the engine fail and my mind would fill with noise again. The car had been a hasty purchase the week I arrived in the college town and an instant demon that needed the attention and money I didn't have.

The bicycle became my salvation. The physical exertion replaced my city walks. I had mapped out favorite routes, favorite times of day, taped a cassette of music to listen to on my tape player and earphones, and set out for hour-long rides. My first month in the college town, I had a session with a local therapist, a woman nearby who advertised in the gay newspaper with a set of initials after her name. When she tried to pin all my problems on my father, I knew I wouldn't return for another session. I wanted to move forward, not dwell in the past. My father's love and/or disinterest wasn't my problem. Things had changed for me. I was struggling with the impact of many deaths. Multiple grief. Survivor's guilt. On my bike rides, I couldn't see the future, but I could see hope for it. I could find ideas, make lists, write paragraphs in my head. And it had become the best therapy I could find to keep me from breaking down.

But I wanted to write about my experiences in the city, with Wade and Mitch and Jesse and Frank, so as hard as I was trying to push them away, I was pulling them back, deconstructing every detail and conversation, and trying to convince myself that I possessed a skill to tell these stories. I wanted to write a novel. My idea was to tell the story of a gay man's journey through the AIDS epidemic, but when I moved to the college town there was no end in sight, just battle after battle, and I distrusted my story to create a protagonist with a happy ending when it wasn't something I was certain that could ever exist. Things felt worse, not better. Instead, I outlined a science fiction tale about a man who arrived on a planet where there was an outbreak of a new virus in the colony, but I realized that I didn't have metaphors and themes and science facts in place to tell this story without a lot of research, and the more I visited the library and read about Mars and space colonies on the moon and the distance to other galaxies, the more I convinced myself that this was not my story to tell.

I wanted to understand my sorrow and grief and my desire to pass through it, so I began assembling notes for an essay until I found my way into writing fiction. It was a story about a gay man who lived in a city apartment whose adventures happened at the last minute when friends contacted him when others were not available. As I worked on this story another story began to take shape as I thought about the times I had been alone in Mitch's apartment after his death and my inventory of his items that would be donated, or sold, or given to his friends and family. Details that revealed Mitch's passions and obsessions, debris that was left behind. There were cast recordings and theater programs and first editions of Maugham and Wilde and Forster novels. There were vintage travel posters and rare, foreign movie posters, some in frames and some rolled up or stacked away in closets. There were refrigerator magnets and snow globes and souvenirs he brought back from his travels. One shelf had been cleared of books to become a repository of medicines and vitamins and ointments and creams—the large yellow pills he hated taking, the tiny blue one he needed for anxiety, the medicines for thrush and herpes and the antivirals. There was the cream I used to keep his skin hydrated, the ointment to prevent the itching, the drops he needed to keep his eyes fluid.

I found a way to tell a story by having characters move items out of a gay man's apartment after his death. The moment I found my way to the end of the story, at the completion of the first draft, I felt the relief of accomplishment. I knew the story needed more work, but it now existed as something outside of my mind. I didn't know if the story would ever be published—that's not what was important to me. Removing these details from my memory and placing them elsewhere, I was able to reach a temporary peace with grief.

They were part of my path in the college town; I was searching for someone like myself, but also someone who was different, someone to keep me aware and engaged. I tried to learn something about myself from each of them. Joe and I had the same birthday, the same number of brothers and sisters, and drove the same type of car. I met him for dinner at a restaurant on the highway. He was nice and charming, shorter than me, and had thick black hair, a black mustache, and a fair complexion. I spent the night at his apartment and we traded phone messages for days, but the enthusiasm faded for both of us; I found him too flighty to see a second time. He did most of the talking; I wanted more of a balance.

Evan lived close by. We met for drinks at an inn near the college; his letter said he had just moved to the area after breaking off a relationship. He was taller, pudgy, had tiny black eyes, and curly reddish hair. He was a great talker, up-to-date on theater and movies. It was nice to compare notes and to have the sort of conversations I enjoyed in the city. He kept staring at my hands the whole time we were talking. Finally, he said he thought I should think about doing some modeling. He said I had handsome hands; he liked the way the hair grew around my wrists. I asked him if he could tell that I bit my nails. He said yes, but a good manicure would solve that. We spoke on the phone several times, but never got together again. I felt that he talked down to me, as if I were not smart enough or rich enough to understand what he was describing. I never pursued the goal of having my hands photographed.

I met Ted through a dating service that I had belonged to in Manhattan and was expiring at the end of the month. We spoke on the phone for close to six hours before we hooked up. He lived about fifteen minutes from the cottage. He was an outdoorsman type, over six feet tall, blondish brown hair, and liked to fish and ski. After dinner, we went bowling. At the bowling alley he started to chain smoke and turned very competitive. He was determined to beat me. I found it unsportsmanlike, but I became immature and pouty because I kept losing. He called and left a message on my answering machine for a second date, but I didn't call him back because I felt he wanted to overpower me.

Sal was a mistake. The minute I saw him I wanted to leave—and so did he, but we stuck it out for a couple of hours. He was over six feet, well built, had black mustache and a scar that ran diagonally across his face. I met him at the movies. The scar unnerved me. I could smell cigarette smoke on him. Afterward, we had coffee together and he told me he used to do drugs. I didn't run away because I thought he might pull a knife or a gun on me. By the time I left with an impolite goodbye, I was so afraid of him I was shaking.

And then there was Nicky. Nicky was an accountant in the city visiting a friend in the area. I saw him at a nightclub in a nearby tourist town. He had blue eyes, fair skin, a nice physique, and a lot of body hair. That evening, I was trying not to drink. He was cruising everyone in sight and I got tired of watching him. He followed me out into the parking lot when I left and I asked him back to the cottage. When we pulled up by the gate, we got out of our cars and looked up at the stars. He put his arms around me. It was romantic and sexy and I really needed him that night. We spoke on the phone when he got back to Manhattan and he promised to visit me but he never returned. And I did not find him someone I wanted to pursue.

One evening as I was returning from a late bike ride, the phone was ringing as I unlocked the cottage door. It was Jesse calling, angrily addressing me with, "Where were you?"

I thought there was bad news arriving, that Jesse was having another health issue, or that someone we knew had tested positive, or was in the hospital, or was dead, but instead at the end of a long string of rants, Jesse said, "He wouldn't even give me a hand job."

I wanted to laugh because he had delivered the news like a punch line. But Jesse was distressed because his world was divided into "those who had it" and "those who didn't." He didn't want any sympathy from me; he was only calling to vent his anger. Again, I had become a mirror, more sympathetic than the truth.

"Take a break," I suggested. "You are welcome to visit me here anytime."

I knew after I made the offer that I had made a mistake. Jesse said, "What? And run away from my life like you did?"

I knew that defending myself would be another battle. "I didn't run away from your life—or mine," I answered him. "I don't understand why you can't be supportive about this. There wasn't any future for me in New York. I wasn't happy. Why can't you be on my side?"

"Because this—this, whatever you are doing, is not you."

"I met someone," I said. "I want to give it a chance. I thought you might want to meet him and help me decide."

"What? What are you talking about?"

I knew the shift from talking about Jesse's life to mentioning mine was a risky move. I explained to him about the personal ads and responses.

"You've been having sex this whole time?" was Jesse's reaction. There was shock and anger and glee in his response.

"Not with everyone."

"But you want my approval of your life when you aren't telling me anything about it."

He made me feel lousy. Suddenly, I thought I was a terrible friend for not telling Jesse everything about myself. But Jesse never wanted to hear about it. "Because you don't respect it," I answered, knowing my wording was again incorrect. "And you would only make fun of its flaws."

A few weeks before Jesse's phone call, I had received a response to my personal ad from a guy who lived a few miles away. Adrian's letter read, "I'm hoping to find someone with whom I can establish a permanent monogamous relationship." He described himself as thirty-three, 155 pounds, 5'9" tall with a "reasonably attractive face and body." When we first spoke on the phone, I learned he worked for the government in a "back-office position" and enjoyed gardening and working outdoors on his time off.

We met for drinks a few days later at a bar in the college town. Adrian had the authoritarian manner of a disinterested bureaucrat: a cautious manner and a reserved reaction. I thought he was handsome in an underappreciated way, normal, not striking: brown eyes, thick brown hair neatly combed into place, important eyebrows, and a slight overbite. Adrian was reluctant to provide details about his job. "I'm not out," he whispered, as if he were an undercover agent. I tried to be charming and conversational, saying I knew little about gardening and landscaping other than what my parents had made me mow and weed in our yard. My mother loved flowers—she selected and arranged them weekly for the church altar. Adrian was quiet and aloof, leaving me to ask all the questions and pry out his answers. I thought he might warm up, but I also wondered if he was being judgmental. We finally fell into a choppy conversation about music. Adrian liked country music and had never seen a Broadway musical.

On our second date, we went to the movies. I met him at the cinema near the highway. There wasn't much time to have a conversation beforehand; we did not touch during the movie or were otherwise affectionate. We parted afterward in the parking lot. I felt that I was being tested to see if I was reliable—that I would show up as had been arranged. I wasn't expecting another date, but a day or so later Adrian called and asked if I wanted to spend time together on a Saturday. I drove to the house he rented in a nearby village. It was a beautiful day, sunny and bright. He had bought some patio furniture from a local auction house, and I helped him sand and prime it with paint. I kept the conversation going with questions, mostly related to sandpaper and paint and soap and water. We had sandwiches for dinner and watched a videotape of a movie he had rented. There was no kissing or snuggling; we sat on opposite ends of the couch, and when the movie ended, I stood up and said that I should be going.

"You can sleep over," he said. There was no warmth in his voice or pleasure in his expression. "The bed is large enough for both of us."

I realized that he was evading a suggestion of sexual intimacy and he clarified it with adding, "I want to take this slow."

We slept together—no sex, no cuddling, not even touching—he was on his side of the bed and I, on the opposite side. By then I understood that men are complicated creatures, and gay men are never what they seem, that you could have a wonderful conversation and later in bed be surprised by a buffet of fetishes. My sleep was restless that night; I kept waking wondering where I was and then questioning why I was there. In the morning, I was thick-headed and sluggish; my face felt covered with grime and sweat.

I left after a hurried cup of coffee. I was so used to being judged sexually, that I was even more confused about how to consider Adrian. I thought his reticence for sex might have something to do with HIV and the fear of AIDS, though we had both confirmed our negative statuses before we met.

But I wasn't ready to give up. I called Adrian a few days later and invited him over for dinner. He brought a bottle of wine. We made popcorn and watched a movie together. I asked him to stay over—I slept on one side of my bed and he slept on another. He was more talkative, but this time he asked questions. Why did I leave New York? Why did I choose the college town? Had I been in a relationship before? Why was I working for an architect? It felt like a pop quiz and I was failing. Worse, I found myself childish and defensive having to explain my answers.

The mistake I made with Adrian was revealing the idea of him to Jesse—and Maggie. I thought I would be giving my life more relevance, more dignity, more pride, if I announced I was dating someone. Subconsciously I knew Adrian wasn't the right person for me, but I wasn't consciously ready to admit this. I thought I could give it more time. But I was already making more mistakes.

Maggie required less and less of my encouragement as she made her way through the building, going desk to desk, architect to assistant to accountant to draftsman, to practice her Tarot readings. She would return to our overheated workspace in a giddy mood, tuck her cotton skirt between her legs, and spill the gossip she had learned. Edward, the woodworker in the basement who built the three-dimensional architectural design models, was seeing a shrink who specialized in addictions; he had stopped smoking pot and taken up gourmet cooking. Will, one of Greg's draftsmen, had separated from his wife. Paula, the receptionist, was leaving the firm to be a caterer; in the accounting department, there was talk of an employee discrimination case.

One morning when I arrived at my workspace, I found Colleen sitting on my stool talking with Maggie. She was dressed in bright spring colors, distinctly out of season, a necklace of giant stones around her neck, her perfume clogging up our airless room. She smiled and said, "We were just brainstorming about how to make this space more functional."

"Functional?" I asked, seeking out Maggie's deep hooded eyes and detecting her irritation.

"Brighten it up a bit," she said. She cocked her head as if she were talking to a child, or someone of a lower station. Maggie caught the gesture as well, and she swiveled away from Colleen and reached for her journal, which meant she was trying to contain her anger, or rage, or misery, or all of the above. I felt certain a new poem would be read to me later.

Colleen pointed to the dark end of our desks, where the slope of the ceiling cut it off. "We could recess some lights along here," she said. "Make it cheerier. Warmer."

"You want to make it warmer up here?" The astonishment in my voice made her stand up and relinquish my stool. "Are you nuts?" I added. "There is no air up here. There is no ventilation system that works. There is no circulation. So your idea to solve this is to add more lights?"

I could tell she didn't like being challenged by someone she felt was beneath her status, but someone from downstairs had obviously sent her up here to find a solution. I realized that this was probably how it originally came to be a workspace—the famous brand-name architect had sent an intern up the stairs with the task of making the tiny space beneath the eaves into something unique—a one-of-a-kind workspace where no one could work.

"What would make it more...comfortable for you?" Colleen asked.

"How about some real chairs? Office chairs with backs and arms. You have us sitting on stools like we're selling shoes."

She tilted her head again and looked at the space Maggie and I shared. "I don't think you could get two chairs in here," she said.

"Of course not," I answered. "Which is why you have a problem."

I turned away from her, heard her displeasure in the tiny stamp of a foot. She silently pretended to search for other solutions, looking at the height of the walls, the angles of the roof, then finally stomped away.

"Cut her some slack," Maggie said.

"You're on her side?"

"I've been practicing with her. She thinks the Tarot is cool. She wants to design a deck."

"Of cards? Are you crazy? That's dangerous territory," I answered.

Later that afternoon, as the draftsmen pretending to be architects were sending out drawings to be mailed, Greg appeared and leaned over my shoulder. "I understand you scared my wife away," he said.

"Unfortunately, she didn't take her perfume with her," I answered.

He belly-laughed and placed two hands at the top of my shoulders, as if to steady himself, but his grasp lingered and he began massaging my shoulders. He leaned in closer, whispering, "You know I can't comment on that."

At the end of the week, I noticed that the glass bowl of the overhead light in the hallway behind our desks had changed, from the nondescript round white design to a tinted amber one with tiny etchings on the glass. I didn't have a chance to discuss this with Maggie because my desk phone was ringing. It was Jesse calling to tell me that he was planning a future event with a drag queen named Pussy Couture. I had seen Pussy several times at a gay bar in Chelsea—she was short, muscular, funny, and took no hostages. Jesse was the type of writer who sought shock and no applause. They would be working together on an impromptu one-night benefit performance called "Beauty and Disease." The fundraiser was scheduled for late in the fall for a new organization that would help gay men with AIDS. I told Jesse that it sounded like a good combination, though I had a premonition that even if it were for a good cause, a clash of egos could prevent the idea from succeeding.

As I asked Jesse for more details, I could tell that Maggie was eavesdropping, and in a way, it made me feel better, that there was a witness to this ongoing drama. I asked about Jesse's health, concerned that he had the stamina to do something like this.

"I expect you to be there," Jesse answered. "In fact, you can be my dresser, or an usher, or president of my fan club."

Before I had a chance to respond, he added, "By the way, I started AZT today. I have to take a pill every four hours. Just another thing you can avoid." And then he hung up.

Maggie was waiting to be supportive, or for me to satisfy her own need for attention. She swiveled her stool and gave me a maddening stare. "Want me to read your cards?" she asked, clutching a large wave of her hair. "Your energy is off balance and it's gonna make me psychotic."

One of the most romantic evenings I have had was with Mitch. We went to the one-ring circus that performed in the winter in the heated tents outside Lincoln Center, something we had done many times in our friendship, but this time Mitch had AIDS. He had Kaposi's sarcoma and had lost a great deal of weight; he had stopped reviewing performances and only went out to something he felt he would enjoy. He wanted to see the acrobats and trapeze acts, studying "the moments they defy gravity and fly and float." That evening, Mitch had trouble walking, afflicted by inexplicable pains in his lower back and legs. The pavement was slippery, covered with snow that had melted and turned to ice. Mitch refused to use a cane and we walked slowly to the entrance of the circus, our heads lowered to the ground, cautious of the surface. It was cold. A brittle wind blew around us. My hands were shoved into my coat pockets for warmth. I glanced up for a moment, noticing the tiny white lights in the trees near the entrance gate. Mitch slipped his arm into mine, his hand resting on the inside of my elbow. At first, I thought this was to balance himself, or to slow down our pace. But then he said, looking ahead, "Isn't it romantic?"

Months later, there was a moment when I was at Adrian's apartment: I was seated on the couch. Adrian was in his kitchen. The afternoon sun was burning bright and warm through a window and I felt sleepy. As I fought off the heaviness around my eyes, I thought of Mitch. A square patch of light warmed a small section of the floor rug and a thought about Maggie's cosmic enthusiasm filled me with awe. I wanted to believe that Mitch was still with me, watching over me. I wanted this to be a sign from him that it was okay to move on, to stop grieving, but I knew it was only a patch of light.

I don't like making comparisons, but that is the inevitable disappointment of life. As much as I hated Mitch, hated watching him become sick, Mitch needed me and I needed Mitch. Adrian had no use for me. There was no desire to accommodate me into his life. We had never had sex together. When I left the apartment all I could think was, "What am I doing? What am I doing?" I felt certain I was making another mistake.

One afternoon I called Adrian at his office—the famous architect had been given a free block of tickets to a performance of touring musicians who were playing at the campus theater and a pair of tickets had filtered down from the architects to the staff to me and I thought about asking Adrian to join me. Adrian's tone was brusque and dismissive when he answered. "I told you this is not a good place for me to talk," he whispered, "Why did you call me here?" and when I repeated that I had gotten free tickets for this evening, he said he could not attend, and added, "I'm going to be out of town this weekend," as if he expected that I would next ask if he wanted to get together later in the week. I asked him if everything was all right; he brusquely ended the call with a nervous sounding, "of course, but I can't talk here."

I went to the concert alone—it was a quartet of string musicians accompanying a cabaret performer singing in French—and as the week went by, I began to sift through more responses to my personal ad, ready to move on from Adrian. I spoke with a couple of guys on the phone and on the weekend; a graduate student I had arranged to meet at the campus bookstore came back to the cottage for sex. He had ice blue eyes and a nervous temperament and I knew when we met, he wasn't interested in a conversation or friendship, only a hookup—he had a thick cock and seemed to want to show it off to someone, so I obliged and toyed with it till he reached an orgasm.

After he left the cottage, I went out on a long bike ride and stopped at the video store on Main Street to find a rental for the evening. I was looking through a shelf of titles when I saw Adrian enter the store. Our eyes met and I felt my face flush with surprise, but I looked away when I saw he was with another fellow—taller, but dressed like he was. I was more relieved than angry—if he was to lie about going out of town, what else would he find to lie about?

Adrian made no movement to say hello, and I made my way to a section of the store that was partitioned with a wooden gate and a sign that read "Adults Only." I looked through the titles until I was hopeful that Adrian had left. There was a two-for-one video rental deal for the night; one of my rentals was porn.

One afternoon I had an odd conversation with Maggie's husband Bryan. It was a Saturday and I had been biking that morning and stopped by Maggie's house at her insistence—she lived a few blocks from the architect's Colonial remodeling mishap in a rented ranch-style house. She was throwing her stepson Luke a sixteenth birthday party and pleaded to me to drop by the house to make sure that she was still sane and functioning. "You have to save me from my mother," she pleaded, then added: "And you have to save me from becoming my mother."

By the time I arrived the teenagers were huddled in a group at the farthest point of the lawn from the house and the adults were seated in the chairs nearest the table of food and drinks. It was always startling to me how beautiful Maggie was when I saw her out of the office. She had braided her hair and was wearing strands of wood bead necklaces over a wrap dress.

"Do you perform in this?" I asked her when she greeted me.

She swayed and rocked her head and smiled. "I prefer leather when I sing," she said. "This is for discovering auras."

We had a brief conversation about the salads, which seemed to have created an argument with Maggie's husband Bryan because they had been store bought and not made fresh in the kitchen, "even though I made all the dips myself," she added. "Not only must I be beautiful, I have to be a domestic goddess," she added, failing to mask her bitterness.

Bryan appeared and shook my hand, tapped me on the shoulder and led me away from the salad table and into the house.

Bryan was tall and about eight years older than Maggie, which would put him into his early forties, and he had that magnetic look of a preppy boy gone to seed from too much booze and fun. I thought he had too much hair for a man his age—slicked and parted but with a strategic floppy strand that batted his right eye. I followed him into the room he used as his office. It had been the largest bedroom in the house, and was now filled with the same sort of business equipment that Maggie and I shared in the architect's attic. I complimented Bryan on his drawings. His graphics were bold and cool, as if he had been raised on comic books.

Bryan closed the office door and I was suddenly worried about his desire for intimacy and could sense myself frowning. He fumbled through a small wooden box on a shelf and found a joint and a lighter and I realized his intent was to keep this activity out of sight of the teenagers—and Maggie.

As he took his first toke of a joint of marijuana, I relaxed my concerns and asked him how he started drawing, and he replied he had taken art classes since grade school, but his turning point was at twenty-one, when he hitchhiked with friends to the Woodstock music festival and filled a journal with sketches and ideas. He went into detail about his drawing of Janis Joplin he had framed on the wall, and at the end I asked him if he had ever seen Maggie perform with her rock band. "Before my time," he answered. "I've heard her classical repertoire," he said. "She still walks over to her mother's house and practices piano."

He handed me the joint and I took a tentative drag. "And she's teaching now," I said, to be part of the conversation. "That must be good."

"It distracts her," he answered. "For a bit." I handed the joint back to Bryan and watched him smoke. Then, after a pause, he said, "But it doesn't replace therapy."

"Therapy?"

"That's how we met. Group meeting."

"Isn't that against the rules?"

"Not really. Not if you're in love." He smoked some more, then said, "I went because of my divorce. Maggie has deeper issues. She's not focused. She jumps from one thing to the next. From the music to the poetry to this silly thing about Tarot cards and predicting the future. Now she wants a baby. When we got married, she had no desire to have children. Neither of us did. Luke has been a handful for me. I don't want any more kids. And what happens when she loses interest in a baby and jumps to the next thing to keep her distracted? What happens to the kid?"

"It might be different—with her being a mother."

"She needs someone to talk it out with."

"Maybe she needs a new therapist."

"She says she doesn't need one," he said. "Because you don't need one."

"Me? What's this got with me?"

"She's using you as a model. She said that you stopped therapy."

I was surprised by this. After a moment, I explained my aborted therapy session when I first arrived in the college town, just as I had told Maggie one day in our overheated office space, an anecdote that I felt certain Bryan was already aware of.

I was lightheaded and stoned, and suddenly paranoid that Bryan was blaming me for being the cause of Maggie's behavior, which on the surface did not seem any more erratic or neurotic than my own. I reached for the door knob and opened the door, hearing myself say, "I don't discourage her. Nothing I do stops her from being who she is or who she wants to be."

I made my way through the house and into the bright sun of the patio. Maggie had made her way over to the cluster of teenagers and I caught her attention and waved goodbye.

I was too wobbly to ride away, so I walked a few blocks pushing my bike, then tried to ride, and decided to continue walking. I felt as if I had been ambushed. Of course, I worried if I had helped steer Maggie into some unnatural path. I began to inventory all of my relationships—with family and friends—hometown, high school, college, and in New York—trying to understand the paths I had chosen and their impact on others. I had a history of disappointing women because of my passive-aggressive behavior, or lack of it—classmates, coworkers, bosses—because I wouldn't allow them the power they wanted over me. My breathing became shallow and I was squinting hard—and I panicked and searched for a place to sit.

I walked into a nearby cemetery and found a bench. I closed my eyes, trying to ease the palpitations that I could feel beneath my eyelids. I remembered calming Mitch one afternoon when he was ill and we tried to make a matinee performance. The theater was only a few blocks away, a walkable journey in good weather, but suddenly now impossible for him to do. But he was insistent and began hyperventilating out of frustration. "Just focus on your breathing," I told Mitch. "In and out. Slow—slow—slow."

We breathed together; my face pressed close to his. When he was calm, we began walking again, my arm offering him support. I remember thinking: Why had I let this happen? Why hadn't I suggested a wheelchair? Why hadn't I tried to talk him out of leaving his apartment? Was I to blame for this? Or was I just trying to help someone out?

I sat on the cemetery bench until I remembered the water bottle attached to my bike frame was empty and decided to bike some more—my goal a simple one—to find water. Take care of myself. Move forward, not back.

"I'm making my doctor pay for this call," Jesse said. It was late afternoon and my work bin was full of "to do" projects, but Maggie was away from her workspace and I needed a break.

"What's wrong?"

"He's a dreamboat, but he's still gouging me and my insurance company. So, I asked the receptionist how to get an outside line and voilà, here you are, on his dime."

"Why are you at the doctor?"

"Aerosolized pentamidine," he answered. "I get it every two weeks."

"For what? What are your symptoms?"

"I have nicknames for my remaining T-cells," Jesse answered. "But I can't remember what they are short for. I might sponsor a contest for suggestions."

This was Jesse, avoiding a serious response. "Let me know where you want me to mail my list," I said.

"I am only taking suggestions from men on the street," he replied. "Ninth Avenue, to be specific. 42nd Street to 59th."

"Once again you are overlooking the entire gay demographic south of 14th Street."

"How do you think I found this doctor?"

Before I had a chance to reply, Jesse added, "My social event of the week was a cocktail party at a penthouse in Chelsea. Trendy fags and dykes full of sperm and anger. I met an editor who wants me to string all my little rants into a book."

"It's a great idea."

"But you've already destroyed my dream."

"How did I do that?"

"I have to find minions to read my work instead of my underlings."

"I thought the group was still meeting."

"You took the joy with you when you left."

There had been five other gay writers, including Jesse, when I joined his writing group, but it was clear to all of us that Jesse was the star in the making. There was a retired teacher working on a revision of *Wuthering Heights* where both lovers were gay, a short, stocky young guy from New Jersey working on a story of a closeted realtor who moonlights as a 42nd Street hustler, a lanky poet with long hair who wrote about his tricks, and a dark-haired writer from Virginia who read excerpts from his sex diary. Jesse had the instincts of a stand-up comic and an improvisational actor. And an undeniable raw and offensive writing talent. He was both his protagonist and antagonist. He didn't show much encouragement or praise to other writers, and as the writing group continued to meet and evolved, I was grateful that he often took a hands-off approach to my own stories, escaping his bitterest remarks, though it meant I spent hours writing notes of encouragement in the margins to the other writers so they wouldn't abandon the group.

"I need some more sex scenes," he said. "So get busy."

"So you would sell your soul to steal my stories."

"My life is a revolution," he said. "And you are avoiding your life. That's what matters."

"I'm not going to let you make me feel guilty today."

"What happens when someone asks you why you weren't there? Why you didn't respond to the call to be part of history."

I was on Jesse's side, I was always on Jesse's side, but I was also weary of Jesse's holier-than-thou stance of putting me down because I wasn't an in-your-face activist and I had left the city. "Why are you minimizing my life?" I asked too harshly. There was anger in my annoyance. "Where were you when Mitch was sick? I don't remember you offering to help after you heard gory detail after detail."

"I was fighting for my own life."

"If that's how you see it. I can answer the same. I fight for my life every day. I fight to pay my rent, to buy food, to try to keep from going crazy. But I know I'm not alone. I try to help someone when they need help."

"And how do you see my life?"

"I see you joining an attention-seeking cult of rowdy, hyper-sexed militants to find yourself a boyfriend, or the next trick, or at least a coconspirator and confidante and fellow advocate for yourself, which is even more attention seeking, while ignoring a friend because he happened to be the one who was sick and needed help. You couldn't even pick up his medicine for him."

Jesse was silent. I knew I had hit a vein. "You forget. He hated me," he said.

"He didn't hate you. He hated everyone."

"Well, gee, thanks for making me feel on top of the world. Go fuck yourself." And he hung up.

But he was back on the phone with me the next day. "I met with Pussy. She thinks the monologue I wrote for her is too angry."

"Does she want you to tone it down?"

"I told her no changes. She called me egotistical."

"I would agree with that."

"And a narcissist."

"True."

"She's fine with me being a bitter queen, but she wants to be warm and fuzzy and funny."

"Is she the beauty or the beast?"

"That's just it," Jesse said. "You're not supposed to know. It's true performance art."

"You hope."

"She wants to lip synch her part."

"What?"

"She says it's what she does. It's her brand. It's what her audience will expect."

"She's got a point."

"I'm not writing Dusty Springfield songs."

"Pity," I answered. And then I lightly laughed.

"What was that?" Jesse asked.

"What?"

"Was that a laugh?"

When I didn't answer, he said next, "Who are you sleeping with?"

I stayed silent.

"Fess up," he said. "You're an egotist and a narcissist on a path of self-destruction."

"You are not talking to yourself in a mirror," I said. "Even sarcasm has consequences."

Jesse sighed. "For a drag queen she is perversely slow. She thinks we must rehearse every movement."

"What comes first?" I asked. "Book or play?"

Jesse stayed quiet and I realized what he was thinking. "I come first," he answered. "How could you forget?"


I am aware that I am writing my survival story and not a love story. I realize that I knew so little of Mitch's life. In the days after his passing, I was surprised to hear from people I never knew or knew existed: a bookstore owner where Mitch brought his used books for resale; the travel agent Mitch used to book trips; an artist who had painted a portrait of Mitch that was at his parents' house; Mitch's classmate from his prep school in Bryn Mawr. At the funeral home on the Upper West Side, a cousin from Philadelphia appeared and asked if Mitch still possessed a sofa that he had acquired from their grandmother because she had always admired it. There was a closed coffin in the room "to offer visitors comfort and closure," even though Mitch had insisted on cremation and an urn with his ashes was hidden in my backpack. People went up to the coffin with morose expressions, touched it, kissed it, whispered words, and left. Strangers rose and told funny remembrances and anecdotes I had never heard before. A coworker at the magazine where Mitch wrote, an elderly woman with dark black eyeglasses and a thick Brooklyn accent, insisted to the crowd that we remember Mitch as an insightful writer. I sat in the hard seat of a folding chair. Jesse sat beside me, whispering in my ear that people were talking too long and when it was his turn to die, he didn't want anyone to speak more than a minute. I thought about the time Mitch confessed to me that he met a Puerto Rican fellow in Times Square and had sex with him in his editor's office and I kept wondering, was that it? Was that when he got it? A neighbor of Mitch's mother approached me and asked, "Why didn't he tell anyone? Why didn't I know about this?" I had no answer for her. I realized I didn't know who Mitch was, I only knew pieces of him, and those few pieces still didn't add up to make me love him. And whatever story I was to write about him would be my story of him, my impressions of him, and not his story.

I finished the draft of a story I had been working on for several weeks. It was based on the time I went shopping with Mitch to buy him a new winter coat. Mitch had become rail thin and his eyes had widened and enlarged into pools of need and fury and his hair had disappeared. Mitch was more difficult then, to the point of being verbally abusive, but the story I wrote about shopping for a coat transformed him into hopeful Broadway dancer fighting off symptoms and infections but eager to return to the stage, the kind of guy one of Mitch's reviews would have ridiculed and destroyed.

But the search for memories—and my desire to change them—were making me more depressed. I couldn't shut off my brain when I went to bed, and I thought of more details, of things that could have been different. I was taking my memories and shaping them into a narrative that never happened.

Mitch as protagonist. A nicer, more noble person. Or was I merely recreating the Mitch that others knew? Had I never seen Mitch as who he was?

I did not have much hope that these stories would be published. So far, I kept getting boilerplate rejections from editors with phrases handwritten on them like "keep trying" and "sorry" and I wondered how long I could handle the rejection. But I printed out more copies of my stories and dropped them in the mail at the post office to magazine editors, hoping, at the same time, that there might be a letter in my post office box from someone I needed to meet, or at least, someone who wanted to meet me.

I have memories of laughing with Maggie; one day in the office she read me scathing haikus she had written describing the architects we worked for and asked me to guess their identities. Another time, we set the clocks an hour ahead hoping that we could leave early.

One weekend in late summer we drove to a parking lot outside a strip mall near the highway. Luke, Maggie's stepson, wanted to learn how to drive a car with a manual transmission and Maggie had volunteered my car as a training tool. Luke had read a manual and studied illustrations on how to shift gears, but we laughed when he tried to figure out the clutch and the brake and then the false starts and the car stalling out and then our dismay when the car really stalled out and couldn't be restarted. I had to walk to a service station and call for a tow truck to have the car repaired. Luke took control of the errors and the breakdown, but I was embarrassed at the wide range of emotions and disbelief I displayed in front of a teenager I didn't know, even to the point of saying to Luke, "I bet your father never loses his cool like this."

We sat at a diner while the car was being repaired; our conversations were long and varied that day, from F. Scott Fitzgerald and the flapper era to John F. Kennedy's politics and ambitions to how to remove rust from patio furniture. Though Maggie had not traveled with her deck of cards, it was inevitable to keep the Tarot out of sight and out of our conversations. Bryan had forbidden—no, forbid was too strong a word—had discouraged Maggie from practicing her readings with Luke—because he was a boy, a teenager, "too young to hear someone telling him what his life might be." They laughed at their conspiracy behind his father's back.

"I predict that the car will be fixed and we will all return home safe," Luke said and laughed and the deep pitch of his voice caught my attention. I remembered my teenage years when I used my first car to escape my family and a girlfriend who was determined to make me give up my independence. I often drove into the countryside, the rural areas just beyond the suburbs, taking a side road or a dirt one and hoping I would become lost and alone, showing up hours later with the excuse that I "took the wrong turn."

Maggie had used her napkin to write the stanza of a new poem. "Wisdom is never easy," she read out loud. "Memory makes it sweeter."

I remember having a thought that day, that Maggie and I were not that far ahead in life to be teaching others, and then another thought, how far ahead in life so many others our age already were, how at my age my parents already had four children and had purchased a house and had a steady income, financial responsibilities, and investments. My younger sister was married and had just given birth to her first child.

"But what lessons have been learned?" I said to Maggie. "How do we move on after this?—That's what you need to add."

Luke was a Leo, which wasn't a surprise; he seemed to be the responsible adult amongst us that day. He had seen the service station. He found the diner. It was intoxicating listening to him talk because I tried to understand how his mind was working and how disruptive the teenage growth hormones could be.

"I've seen Jupiter through a telescope," he said at one point.

"His school has some of Einstein's equipment," Maggie added.

I heard Mitch's voice ringing through my mind, "Everyone sees the world differently. I can only tell you my point of view."

It began to rain outside the diner and I sensed a shift in our temperaments; suddenly, we were all anxious for the day to be over. Maggie shut down first, scribbling on a napkin, searching through her purse. Luke disappeared into his own thoughts. After an hour, I walked to the service station and used an overextended credit card to pay for the car repairs.


Late in the month, I received a response to my personal ad from a guy who had just moved to the college town. His note was short and read like his own ad: *New to area, GWM, 35, professor. Enjoys music, theater, movies, reading. 6 feet, 145 pounds.* When we first spoke on the phone, I learned Stuart had recently moved to the college town from Boston, and, like myself, was adjusting to life in a small-town environment. We met for brunch a few days later. The major complication, I found out on our first date, was that he had left a floundering relationship with a lover back in Boston, but he emphasized he was moving on from it.

Stuart was dark-haired and slender, with a stiff posture, narrow shoulders, long, thin arms and wide hands. His brown eyes were hidden by wire-rim glasses that sat atop a nose too large for his face. He reminded me of the tenured professors I disliked when I was in college, snobbish, aloof, and authoritarian. I asked him back to the cottage after brunch and he stayed the night. His enthusiasm, when it bubbled over, seemed out of character for a rigid disciplinarian, particularly in the bedroom. I don't want to emphasize the sex because we shared other interests. He was smart and could articulate why he loved a particular book or song or movie. He loved the theater, particularly musical theater, and he had strong opinions on Sondheim as a talent without peers. I knew enough from having worked in the theater and having sat through some awful performances with Mitch to be able to challenge him on every lyric and inverted melody he loved and adored and thought fabulous to prove that his opinion might only be his own (or not as balanced as it should be).

"I don't know why I even took the job here," he complained the first night at the cottage as he was thumbing through my record albums. Stuart had accepted a newly created professorship at the college teaching Latin. "The department doesn't do musicals. The Dean says it would give the wrong impression. Back in Boston musicians trained to be actors and actors to be musicians. We had a Gilbert and Sullivan Society that was a major fundraiser. You just can't ignore the *faygelahs* and their show tunes and get away with it!"

"Why would the Latin department do musicals?" I asked.

"I'm a multi-disciplinarian," he answered. "That's why they hired me. I can teach core Latin and other courses—Etymology, Classics, Greek drama."

"History of the Broadway Musical?"

"I plan on making myself indispensable."

I liked that Stuart was a determined overachiever, strongly opinionated, argumentative, and stubborn, because it kept me awake and on my toes. Stuart's arrogance spilled over into other topics; menus for meals, ingredients for cocktails, the best way to sear a steak, what to add to a salad to give it a special kick. It felt as if were all too studied, as if a mentor had rapped these ideas over and over until Stuart believed in them. But there were certain topics off limits, specifically any questions about his ex-lover Hal.

"How long were you together?" I asked him one night.

"Too long."

"That's not much of an answer," I said. "Where did you meet him?"

"I don't want to share this," he answered defensively. "This is private."

His tone was sharp and firm. I nodded and changed the subject.

Of course, I wondered what the issue was. Stuart liked us to sleep nude, his taller frame spooning my body, another thing that required an adjustment of me. What made Stuart distinct was that he was one of the few men I had dated who weren't entirely interested in his own orgasm. He wasn't satisfied until I had finished too, a trait I misinterpreted over and over.

By the end of the first week, we had spent every other night together and I was suddenly in some kind of a relationship. I didn't know how to explain it because I didn't understand what I wanted from it or where it was going. And I didn't know what Stuart wanted or expected. Something didn't feel right—I liked being with him, but I wasn't sure I liked him, but I talked myself out of abandoning the hope that it could become something more significant.

Jesse called me one night after midnight. The phone rang several times before I picked up, and I had to stop the answering machine message before I could hear him. His voice was high, strained, and loud, too loud for someone after midnight: "He's gone! Twenty of us marched out of the meeting and started chanting down 13th street but we didn't know where to go so we just ended up in Abingdon Square just chanting and screaming. That fool boyfriend of his wanted us all to get arrested for disturbing the peace but I bought into his pain and then I was screaming at him for trying to set us all on fire!"

I tried to get him to stop talking, and finally got him to listen to my interruption. "What is it? What happened?"

"Tommy Gunn," he said. "Tommy Gunn is dead. There is no way out of this. It's a one-way ticket to hell."

I tried to get Jesse to back up, to tell me the whole story. This was what I had been able to put together: Jesse had gone to the Monday night ACT UP meeting and Tommy Gunn's lover had interrupted the proceedings, stood up and announced that Tommy was dead and demanded that the group take immediate action, that now was the time to act out, not a week later, not a month later, not at a planned demonstration, but now. That if they were arrested tonight, it would be tomorrow's news and they had to be arrested again, to keep the story alive and to honor Tommy Gunn's legacy.

He'd elicited a fear in Jesse, a fear that there was no path to health, that an AIDS diagnosis was a terminal one. "Jesse, this stress is going to make you worse," I said. "The anger is going to do more bad than good. Make you sick. *More* sick."

I didn't know if I was right or wrong. I didn't know what path Jesse should take. I only thought that he would never regain his strength unless he let go of his rage.

"You are so wrong," he said. "I don't know why I even called you."

He slammed the phone down and I was left in the dark, disturbed, and feeling like I had failed.

My heart was racing. My instinct was to pick up the phone and try to continue the conversation, but I knew that it would only fuel the animosity. I wasn't ill. Jesse was.

I drank some water, glanced out the window of the cottage. It was a clear night, but windy, and I could see the branches of the trees on the far hill swaying. I wanted to physically react, put my body into motion to calm it down. It was too dangerous to bike at night. I stepped out on the small deck and looked up at the stars. I imagined myself moving, floating, flying. I wanted to understand what this was all about, at the same time wishing I knew how to find the constellations and admonishing myself for not being smarter, for not trying harder. I always felt I never did enough. So I looked again at the swaying branches. And then went inside and tried to fall asleep. Something that eluded me that night.

Stuart set our agenda. He had a teaching schedule that meant a lot of office hours and meetings outside of his classes. I found his enthusiasm to succeed at the college amusing, though his superiority complex could make me feel like an imposter as an adult. By the end of our third week dating we fell into a routine of meeting for dinner on Wednesdays and Saturdays, sometimes at a restaurant, other times we would cook at the cottage. He stayed the night at my place; we seldom were together at his apartment; and he left the following morning, though on Sundays he might linger and read through the sections of the *Times* and lecture me with his commentary on current topics.

One evening he showed up to the cottage with a record album. He flashed it in front of my face and said, "Guess who's going to the opera?"

It was a 1974 recording of the opera *La Bohème*. "It's not the best recording," he said. "The best was the 1955 studio recording."

He put the album on my stereo and we listened to it as we cooked and ate. Stuart changed from a comic, stork-like professor into a fluid, animated conductor, lifting his arms up in tempo, tapping out the beats with his fingertips. The following evening, Stuart and a colleague from his department, were driving to Manhattan to see a live production of the opera.

"I was an intern as a rehearsal prompter for a production in Boston," he said. "Every day, I was a wreck but it was worth the experience."

I was pleased to see that he was in a good mood. "Jealous, aren't you?" he asked as we were cleaning up.

"I'm not a huge fan of the opera," I admitted.

"What?" he asked. "Who are you not to think this is heaven?"

"I had a friend in the city who hated opera. That might have rubbed off on me some."

"This staging is supposed to be radical," he said. "Three quarters. Almost in the round. The sound is supposed to be magnificent."

He gloated the rest of the evening. I was jealous of the glee and joy he displayed of the adventure, and it made me feel left out and disconnected.

After Stuart shut me out of knowing anything of Hal, I did not share details with him about Jesse or Maggie; I referred to them as "my friend in the city" or "my coworker." Stuart didn't seem interested in knowing more details of them, or of knowing of my prior life in Manhattan or boyhood growing up with my family. He didn't ask about my writing—what I was at work on, why I was writing fiction. He was a performer in front of an audience of one.

But I was also at fault; I did not speak of Stuart with Jesse or Maggie; I think, perhaps, because I did not trust our relationship to continue. But I convinced myself I was still learning to like Stuart— the sex was good, maybe too good. I was learning more about Latin. And etymology. And Greek history. And men. And I had come to desire Stuart holding me as we slept; his body was a comfort and I missed him when he wasn't around.

I don't understand the stars, or astrology, or horoscopes, or birth charts, though I am aware that often when one thing becomes blissful, another thing may fall out of balance and become a source of pain. Maggie was upset when I arrived at our work alcove. I saw that the notebook on her desk space was full of dark scribbles. She lifted her head from her journal when I asked her if she was all right. "I can't do this," she said.

I thought she was being overdramatic, crying out for attention, but the page in her journal looked disturbing. It was covered with deep, angry, black lines. "Do what?" I answered.

"*This.*"

She pushed the top stack of Tarot cards next to her toward my desk space.

"Misery and abuse," she said. "Card after card. It's turning me into a liar. I can't lie to someone when I pull the Hanged Man or the Devil. I thought if I told people about their lives, I would be hopeful and inspirational and I would be happy helping them find a path forward because that would be helping me. But there's no hope and inspiration. There's no joy. Not for anyone. I pull these cards and I have to lie to the people who see them, who know that I am lying and a fool and a loser... What was I thinking?"

"I'm sure it's like any talent," I said. "It takes practice to be impartial to someone else's story."

"It's too dangerous," she said. "When I perform a song, I'm taking something finished and interpreting it. These—these cards are telling you a story that hasn't happened yet."

"And might not happen," I said. "You can't see the future. You know that. You are just telling someone something that they may want to hear."

"You don't get it," she said. She clutched a handful of her hair and tugged at it. "I need this to make me feel better."

"I don't know anyone who has had their fortune told and felt better."

I realized I wasn't doing a good job of lifting her spirits. "You're helping someone prepare for the future."

"Alan called me into his office last night," she said.

"He wanted a reading too?"

"No," she said. "He told me to stop doing readings while I am at work. It's making everyone in the building upset."

"That's crap," I answered. "Maybe there's a poem in this. You could write a poem. Have you sent any of your poems out to be published?"

"You're being cruel," she said. "You're not taking me seriously."

"I am," I answered. "Your poems are good. Your card readings are good because you see the truth and you want to be honest. You shouldn't beat yourself up because of it. Maybe if you did something different, use what you learned in your poetry, the readings will seem more natural to you when you go back to them."

We worked in silence for a few minutes. I could feel Maggie's mind at work. The air was stifling. It seemed to get hotter and hotter and I felt flushed. In my mind, I replayed my conversation with Bryan, Maggie's husband. I should have used this opportunity to press her about returning to therapy, about starting up again with a therapist. Instead, I asked her, "Did Alan agree to another fan for us?"

Maggie looked at me like I was mad. She got up from her chair and went into the bathroom. I heard her turn on the water at the sink. And then my phone rang.

I could see the mistakes I was making but I convinced myself that they weren't mistakes. I hadn't planned to keep the trip to Manhattan a secret. The journey was a little over ninety minutes by train. Mentally, it was like traveling to another country. Stuart had been willing to drive to the city, but I wasn't ready for that sort of trek and I said it would be less stressful to take the train. He wanted to see a matinee performance of a Sondheim revival off-Broadway. I didn't want to incur the cost of an overnight hotel room, so we both considered it a short day trip.

We left early on a Saturday morning. We ate lunch at a diner on West 46th street before the performance, then walked to the theater. After the show, we walked down Ninth Avenue to catch a train back to the college town.

I had not confided to Stuart about the loss of Mitch and Wade and Frank and the others I had known when I had lived in the city. But more curiously, Stuart asked me no questions about my life in Manhattan. Where did I live? When did I move here? What parts did I like? What did I hate? I was using Stuart to sweep me away from my grief and fear. Stuart was using me as a companion to his next adventure. I tried to convince myself I was returning to the city as a tourist, but as we made our way through midtown, I noticed too many changes—a store that had closed and another that had been replaced, the change of the name of a restaurant, and a bar that was boarded up. As I walked beside Stuart, I fell deeper into myself.

And I was unprepared to find myself moving though grief again. There were too many people— riders on the train, pedestrians on the street, audience members at the show. The dead were everywhere—in the sleeve of a shirt, the scuff marks on a shoe, the profile of a nose, the color of eyes, the part of a man's hair. I noticed glimpses of Mitch. One guy looked like Frank. Another man had Wade's expression.

We were back in the cottage that evening. Because it had been a short, day trip, carefully orchestrated by Stuart, I had not told Jesse that I would be in the city. I was exhausted from the stress. The entire day I had been consumed by guilt, as if I were to run into Jesse at any moment and would have to invent a lie about why I was in New York again.

When Stuart left the next morning, I went for a long bike ride. I was grateful that Stuart, like Adrian before him, had no interest in biking. It gave me the time to unravel many of my uncertainties. I realized our conversations were not conversations. Stuart was all statements and opinions—there were never any conversations. It started to rain when I was near a park, and I felt relieved, as if I were a sponge and wringing out all my insecurities.

I've tried to write this story many times, but I always stop when it becomes necessary to admit my own faults and vulnerability. Or now, as though building a case against Stuart or pointing out Mitch's faults and Jesse's imperfections and Maggie's imbalance.

The truth is, no one teaches you how handle life's challenges. I was aware of how lucky I was, but I was also aware of the battlefield where I was lying—I understood that I was a small point in what was becoming a larger historical record—a community facing a disease. An epidemic. There was no guide book to tell you how to be a gay man, or a good person, or a better lover or friend or neighbor, a citizen of the world. Everyone fights differently; everyone grieves differently, at a different pace. I imagined myself as one of those giant air socks outside of a car dealership, wings flapping in the wind to garner attention.

I was also pinned by my own fear—a fear of testing positive, of having AIDS, of dying, and not having achieved anything except to mourn the person I wasn't. Even though I wasn't infected, the virus was shaping my life, influencing my decisions.

I was envious of the architects, and Stuart, and Jesse. They had found careers to pursue, goals to reach, a point of pride in themselves. They had shaped a path forward—illness would be an obstacle for them, not a breaking point.

In many ways I thought that Jesse was right; I was living a phony life, I was an imposter in the college town, but not because I had left the city behind. I felt as if I had not been a good enough boy, or man. I thought I had little expertise and experiences—I had not learned enough husbandry and common-sense skills to make my way through life successfully. I couldn't fix anything in the cottage if it were to break—the plumbing, the electricity, the furnace. I didn't understand investments, or economics, urban planning, or farm machinery. My car perplexed and frustrated me. I was increasingly aware of the rise of traffic outside the cottage in the early morning hours—tradesmen in their trucks and vans en route to appointments and repairs. Larger trucks passing by with deliveries and shipments.

I knew I needed something to support myself, other than my belief that I could be a writer. I knew I needed a plan to survive and a goal to achieve. A reliable fallback strategy. But there were times I felt that I had trapped myself into another box. I didn't know what I could do or what I should learn.

Some days, on my lunch break, I would bike to the town library and read—thumbing through magazines and newspapers, copying out quotes from reference books, reading a self-help book, studying maps and photographs for some kind of clue of an unknown mystery. A few days I made my way through a refresher course on the proofreading symbols I had used on a temporary job at a law firm on Wall Street. Perhaps I could be an editor. Another day, I searched out the property records where the cottage was located. Maybe I could become a realtor.

There was a bulletin board near the entrance of the library, which is where I discovered the flyer for the bicycle maintenance class at a bike shop near campus. It was geared for the more serious cyclists who did long country routes and competitive rides, but it offered "tips for students," which I felt included me since I knew little about bike maintenance. I had come to recognize myself as always a student—a learner—never a teacher, nor a role model.

There were about six guys and one girl who attended the evening class. Dan, the instructor and part-owner of the cycle shop, was in his early thirties, tall and lithe with spiky brown hair. He demonstrated how to change a tire, how to repair a spoke, how to fix the chains and repair the brakes. It was a commanding performance—Dan was dressed in a tight lycra biking outfit, sometimes reaching for his helmet or a water bottle or a tool kit he kept in a seat pack. His physique rippled with every motion. It was like watching a porn video and I had to knock myself away from staring at him too intently— regarding the others in the class watch him without blinking or breathing.

Dan was a smart teacher—referring to each of us by our names. I wanted to be his instant best friend and boyfriend and lover, but I knew from my prior experiences that he was the type of guy who would swallow me up and move on to the next one—sexually or otherwise—and I would be left depressed and alone.

After the class, I bought a seat pack for the bike at the house. Dan was working the register and held my gaze and handed me his card. "We should go biking sometime," he said.

I called Jesse when I returned to the cottage. "Who are you sleeping with this week?" he answered, with a laugh in his voice. And then I told him about Stuart. And the bike class with Dan. And we were as giddy as schoolgirls.

"It's not good," Maggie said, when I showed up to work. She was seated on her stool, her hair scooped up because of the heat, and I could glance into the top of her blouse and see the shape of her breasts. She had complained many times that the guys in the office appeared at her desk just to leer and stare at her but at that moment, I wondered if she provoked the attention. I soon learned that she'd had a fight with Bryan. He had told her again that he didn't want another child; he'd been through too many custody issues with his ex-wife.

The fight had occurred Friday evening and the next morning Maggie had gotten up early and driven to Baltimore. She had made contact with Chip, her old boyfriend from San Francisco who was an amateur astrologer. Chip had drawn out Maggie's natal chart and given her a detailed reading of it. "You must always be able to do what you wish, no matter what," he had told her, "You're stubborn if someone tries to force you into a mold."

"Doesn't sound good for your marriage," I told Maggie, when she had explained her planetary alignment to me.

"My Moon is fifteen degrees into Aquarius," she said. "Not a good place. Chip was very comforting and sympathetic."

"So you slept with him?"

"Of course not," she answered, reaching her hands above her head and unclipping her hair, then twisting her hair tighter and reclipping it. Next, she shook her head, as if testing the clip, and kept her face at an angle and added, "Well, yes. Kind of."

"Kind of?"

"Let's not get into details."

Then she mentioned that she had not had a cigarette or a drink since she came home, which I thought meant the trip had made her full of remorse. "Chip was cool. He made me see a lot of things about myself," she said. "Karma and consent.

And how I desire emotional self-control and need to practice it."

"With Bryan or motherhood or addiction?"

"All of the above."

As the work on the Hollywood project intensified, Greg's trips to my desk were augmented by those of another architect, a deputy managing fellow named Keith. Keith was a thickly built transplant from the suburbs of Texas who had studied for his design degree in Arizona and looked more like the coach of a high school girls' basketball team than a licensed architect. But he had developed the flat, minimalist execution that the famous brand-name architect embraced and embellished in other architects. As an individual, however, he exhibited more curiosity about his coworkers than the other self-absorbed, anal-retentive designers, who thought themselves a better and more superior class than the office staff assigned to help them achieve their daily tasks. Keith was covered with swirls of black hair traveling up from his fingers and wrists and popping out of the top of his shirt collar. Unlike with Greg, my gaydar went on a blinding alert when he was around, though I knew it was best not to comment or react to it.

Keith always remarked on the battlefield scenarios and heat strokes Maggie and I were often subjected to, as if he were amazed to still find us alive in our little space of horrors. He also took an interest in the town where we worked, quizzing me about a nearby flea market and the local restaurants and music clubs, places he said his wife wanted to visit. I responded the only way I knew how to respond. I said this in a polite way to Keith, emphasizing the places I felt most comfortable— as a gay man—as my way of testing his acceptance, tolerance, or disdain of gay life. I had little desire to engage in polite banter as Maggie did with the rest of the office, and if Keith displayed any objections to my gay life, there was little reason for me to provide recommendations to him about *anything*.

His response, however, surprised me. "I think my older brother once mentioned that place. The dance club."

"Your brother?"

"When he lived on campus."

The inflection of Keith's voice, the mention of an older brother seemed to pitch his recollection into a past I did not wish to inquire further about. Even Maggie, sitting beside me, heard the nuance of his voice, and swiveled around on her stool to consider saying something to Keith.

But she remained silent, too. Keith handed over the work he'd brought for me to do. As he left our workspace, I was thrown into silence and confusion. I didn't want to talk about my experiences and I didn't want to speculate on Keith's older brother, and as I read through the memos and began typing, I thought of myself as selfish.

Time is both the protagonist and antagonist of grief. The days began to shorten, the weather became cooler, the leaves started their spectacular descent into fall. I worried that I had made a series of new mistakes—of moving to the college town, of my continued inability to find and focus on a career that could financially support myself, of falling into a relationship with a guy who seldom knew me outside of the bedroom.

Stuart wanted to return to New York; there was a new Broadway musical he wanted to see. New York seemed so far away to me and the costs of such a getaway seemed frivolous, when I was barely able to pay rent and utilities and keep up with car repairs, but I was grateful that he was arranging the trip with a group of his graduate students—and he did not expect—or secretly want—me to join them. When he left the cottage early that rainy Sunday morning to make a Broadway matinee, I bundled up my dirty laundry and headed to a laundromat. I was seated in a corner, holding a book and a notepad where I was trying to scribble out lines of a conversation of two characters in a story, when I noticed Keith arrive, carrying in a basket of laundry.

I looked back at my notepad, not to be unfriendly, but to give him any space and privacy he wanted, and I didn't want to give myself away. I'd developed a crush on him and found myself studying him as much as I could: the sound of his voice as he stood over me and explained the numerical order of his blueprints, the way his pants rested at his waist, the black stubble of his chin and neck that darkened as the day went on. After he loaded a washer, he came and sat beside me and I smiled in a way that felt unnatural and phony because I was nervous, wanting to make a good impression. He mentioned that the washer and dryer at the house he had rented with his wife hadn't been repaired and I joked that I was just poor and disenfranchised and relied on a laundromat.

He asked if I lived nearby and I told him of my cottage rental and that there was a closer laundromat but it was often filled with students and there was usually a long wait. Because we were sitting side by side, I could only see parts of him— the damp, worn sneakers, the chinos dotted with paint drops, the black hairs that swirled around his wrists and down to his knuckles. I twisted myself to look at him while he was speaking, and to catch his eyes. He mentioned he had driven by the gatekeeper's cottage several times but had not realized that it was where I was living.

We talked a little about Maggie—she'd approached him about a Tarot reading—and I explained her method of practicing on coworkers and Alan's retaliation. "It's a smart trick to break the ice with someone," I said. "Unless the cards become too spooky."

He laughed and said that he had had his fortune told in New Orleans several times. College trips. In Jackson Square. I nodded and added I had once spent a few days in the French Quarter with friends who wanted to go to strip clubs on Bourbon Street. "Not the right place for me," I joked. "I was already broke and in the gutter."

I added that Maggie could catch him up on office gossip. He replied that the office gossip had already made its way to him. "Everyone wants to talk about things they shouldn't be talking about," he said. "I heard you moved here from New York. You don't mind if I ask why you left the city?"

It was a question I was familiar with but could never articulate the same answer twice, because I was hesitant to admit that I was avoiding—or perhaps in the midst of—a nervous breakdown. I wanted Keith as a friend, the sort of friend I'd been unable to find so far in the college town, but I thought it best to remain lighthearted, since Keith's status as an architect outranked my position as "typist in the attic."

"I lived there for a decade," I answered. "I realized I wanted to be someone else."

"And are you?"

"I'm still trying."

My dryer had stopped so I said goodbye and gathered up my clothes. As I was leaving, Keith was loading his wet laundry into a dryer. He said, "Let's have lunch together this week."

On my favorite bike route, I would cycle down the road behind the cottage alongside a field where corn was grown alongside a field of leafy, low vegetables, then I would turn left and ascend a hill, sometimes needing to walk the bike uphill because the incline was too steep for me to pedal. When I reached the small farmhouse where Rick and Sarah lived, there was a road on the right that led to a neighborhood of expensive homes. They were too large and grand and spaced out between each other to call the area a subdivision. The lawns were manicured and meticulously landscaped with hedges and gardens and I often wondered what kind of wealth had purchased these houses. After a mile, there was another road which leveled off between two farming fields and I liked to coast and feel the breeze moving around my body, a hawk usually soaring overhead. By then, after biking for close to forty-five minutes, I would have reached a sweat and a rhythm of pedaling and I would need to make a decision; I would have to convince myself to go further or return to the cottage.

I started creating lists while I was out biking—lists of people who were friends, lists of my family members, lists of places where I worked, lists of birthdays, lists of guys I had dated or slept with, lists of people I knew who had died. It had a therapeutic impression of meaning and pride and validation. I bought a small notebook—the kind Maggie kept at the side of her desk—and when I was back at the cottage, I would write down the lists. And I'd create new ones—lists of things I liked to eat, my favorite books and movies and characters. I would list the stories I had written, the stories I wanted to write, a list of ideas for novels and plays. I broke the lists into further lists—lists of comedies and musicals and most handsome movie stars. I made a list of writers I admired, another list of stories I loved, another list of books I wanted to read and those that I should read. I made a list of what makes a good character, a list of plots, a list of romantic and sexual images. I was using these lists to help define myself.

I had another list of "positive thinking"—not to smoke, avoid alcohol, reminders to exercise and groom and clean the cottage. I had a list of things I liked and things important to me. I had a list of "worry spots" and "causes of stress." I found that writing these lists down, putting thought behind the items on the list, helped the challenge of facing them with a more determined mind.

I seldom shared my lists with others, but they came to be part of the core responses when I spoke with guys who answered my personal ad. They also worked their way into conversations with Jesse. Jesse was a list queen, though his lists were always more outrageous than mine: a list of best asses, a list of things that made him anxious, a list of symptoms, a list of people and companies he distrusted, a list of times he had cried.

It was close to the end of the work day when I reached Jesse at his office desk overlooking Union Square. He answered on the second ring. "I don't want you to be embarrassed or ashamed or upset that you overlooked me on the day I expected you to notice me the most."

"I am the only focus of my attention," he said. "And you are not Oscar Wilde."

"I don't know who I want to be, but it's not Oscar Wilde."

"What is your boyfriend who is not your boyfriend doing for you tonight?"

"He doesn't know," I answered. "I'm avoiding him."

"He's going to be angry when he finds out."

"He'll find a way to blame me for not putting it on his schedule," I answered. "I seem to have a soft spot for egotists and narcissists."

"I've made six new lists today," Jesse said. "They are all about the ways I hate Pussy Couture."

"All art is a challenge. You should make a list of how to get her to like you more."

There was a silence, as if I had hit a nerve. "She's trying to soften my voice, overpower the story so that it is about her and not me."

"I'm sure there's some truth in what she says."

"She's not paying rent for the theater, or finding the ushers, or getting someone to turn the lights on and off. Oh, right, she's getting paid to do this. Pussy for hire. That means she has to say what I want her to say or don't say it all."

"Good luck with that," I said and hung up.


"Gossip is that you are writing a book," Keith said, when we were seated at the picnic table on the lawn near the far end of the parking lot outside the architect's Colonial house mishap.

"I'm always surprised that someone finds me worthy of gossip," I answered. "I had a job in the city where I was accused of sleeping with a coworker, and all I could think of was what a waste of someone's time and energy, because it was none of their business and had nothing to do with our jobs."

"Were you?"

"Of course, but I wasn't even an employee. I was a temp!"

"I'm sure you could write volumes on this place," Keith said.

"You haven't been here long enough to laugh at the dysfunction," I answered. "No one would believe me if I wrote the truth."

"My mom wrote a book," Keith said.

"Was it published?"

"She found a printer who published a few copies for her." After a bite of his sandwich, he added, "It was sentimental. Too sentimental. But sincere."

"A memoir?"

"About my older brother," Keith answered. "He died at home."

I saw a darkness come over Keith's expression. He bent forward, defensively, his shoulders tensing. Even without confirmation, I understood that his brother must have been an early casualty of the epidemic. "How old was he?" I asked.

"This was 1985," Keith said. "He was thirty-eight. The local library wouldn't even accept a copy of the book."

"This was Texas?"

Keith nodded.

"I'm not sure what Maggie has said about my writing," I said.

"As long as it's truthful," he added. "That's what will be remembered."

Saturday evenings in the city when I was alone, when Mitch hadn't called and Wade had other plans and I had no out-of-town visitors, I would walk through the Village streets visiting bookstore after bookstore. I found comfort and hope in books. There was a gay bookstore on Hudson Street where I would look through the new books that had been published or read a passage from a book I couldn't afford to purchase. Someone once told me that you should be like the man you want to meet, so I would stand in the fiction aisles, reading, hoping someone would notice me before I became self-conscious.

There was an "adult bookstore" on Christopher Street, that, if I recall correctly, you had to enter by passing through a turnstile. I'd flip hurriedly through the gay magazines, studying the images of nude men, and glance up at the guys who passed by headed toward a backroom that I was too timid to visit myself.

I'd walk along Christopher Street, trying to determine if anyone was cruising me. I wasn't a type, unless a confused-bookish-boyish-nerd-in-the-wrong-place requires a distinction. I was suspicious of random hookups; sex in public spaces wasn't who I was. There were a couple of restaurants on Bleecker Street that I had been to with friends, sometimes with Mitch, and I'd stand across the street and watch customers arrive and depart. There was another gay bookstore on Christopher Street, and a small bookstore on Tenth Street, opposite the entrance to a gay bar.

For a while I would walk around Sheridan Square—there was a time when there was a men's gym on the second floor of a building, where you could watch guys walking back and forth and barbells rising and lowering. Some nights I would lean against a building and smoke a cigarette. I'd started smoking at gay bars because I didn't know what to do with my hands, but I reached a point where I was self-conscious of looking like someone who didn't look cool while smoking. I never met the man I hoped to meet, usually only someone who wanted to trick. After a while of walking and standing, I would backtrack my steps and go to one of the gay bars and have a drink or two. Later, on my way back to my apartment, I would stop for a slice of pizza—or a donut.

There was an evening I was drinking too hard and fell into a conversation with a guy who bought me another drink. I liked him a lot. But this was during the days after Mitch had died and I had no capacity for anything other than grief. The man walked me back to my apartment and we kissed on the stoop of my apartment building. I don't remember his name. There are times now when I think I never knew his name, only the possibility he represented and the opportunity I let slip away.

The days grew colder. The yellow, orange, and red leaves fell to the ground and became brown. On campus, there were groundsmen raking the leaves into piles, blowing other leaves to the sides of the streets. I hardly ever saw any students.

Maggie announced one morning, "I'm a lousy teacher."

"That's hard to believe," I answered. "With your experience."

She was silent for a while. "That's one of the nicest things you've ever said to me."

"I'm sure there are others," I answered. "Aren't you keeping track of them in your notebook?"

She laughed. "Angelica fired me," she said.

"Fired you? You're teaching her daughter for free. How can she fire you?"

"I yelled at Claire," Maggie said. "Well, not yell, my voice was louder. And unhappy. She hadn't been practicing and she was worse than the week before."

"So you dumped on an eight-year-old."

"I worked so hard when I was that age," she said. "I wish I could get back all those hours I spent practicing."

"To do what? Write nursery rhymes?"

"So it's my fault she can't learn?"

"You can't teach talent."

"So—I'm the one at fault. I'm the one being blamed. It's made me feel insecure," she said.

The daylight grew shorter, though it was hard to tell in our enclosed workspace, unless we left it for another part of the building.

I felt less and less like I was in a relationship with Stuart and more like I had a sex partner who sometimes slept over. His schedule was filled with exams and office appointments. At the last minute, he canceled the luncheon I had planned for him to meet Maggie. "Something's come up," he said, when

I answered the phone, and a day later when I saw him, he dismissed it again with "a student issue." My gut told me he had taken a field trip, either to Philadelphia or New York. Someone had given him a better offer.

Rain fell and the trees were blackened twigs. November ticked by, Then, Stuart called to let me know that he was going to Boston to see his parents.

"During the holiday break for classes," he said. "I need to spend time with them."

I had planned to attempt to cook a Thanksgiving dinner in the cottage and celebrate, but I lost the enthusiasm when I learned Stuart wouldn't be there to participate in my kitchen charade. Maggie asked if I wanted to share Thanksgiving dinner with her and Bryan and Luke and her mother, but I answered her honestly, that I didn't want to be caught up in that sort of awkwardness. She tried to make it sound more inviting, but it was the one thing I knew I had to avoid and she agreed it was destined to be miserable. I had told my parents that I would visit later in December, but my aunt called and asked if I wanted to spend a weekend with her and her second-husband. They lived in the northern part of the state. I made up an excuse that I had promised someone else—an old college friend—that I would spend time with him and asked for a raincheck for another weekend. I checked in with Jesse, on the off chance that he wanted company, but he was now on his own timetable with rehearsals and a schedule of benefit performances during the holiday week. I suffered through a tirade of how he felt that Pussy was trying to sabotage their benefit performance. "She thinks I need to dress better," Jesse whined over the phone. "I told her I was going to do my part in the nude."

"It would sell tickets," I told him. "But it could make you sick."

"I'm gonna turn all the lights up to super bright so she melts."

"That's a bit severe, don't you think?"

"Then I'm going to crank up a wind machine so she's only left with duct tape and a padded bra."

I laughed—and was grateful for the humor, but I also knew that there was a lot of truth to Jesse's comical vengeance.

Mid-week I ran into Keith at the video store. He spotted me and asked for movie recommendations—his wife's sister and her husband were joining them for the holidays and he knew he needed something to escape from all of them. As we were talking about movies, I noticed a tall, good looking guy with spiky hair enter the store. I thought he might be one of the dates from my personal ad—many times I had used the video store as a meeting point, but it was Dan, the bike store owner and instructor. I introduced him to Keith and noticed him weighing whether we were a couple. I felt awkwardly entrapped until one of the video store clerks—a student and fellow biker, I guessed—approached and began talking to Dan, and Keith and I made our way to the register and the sidewalk and said goodbye.

I spent Thanksgiving checking in with my family on the phone, and then, in the afternoon, I drove up the hill to pick up my elderly neighbors. I'd arranged to take them to a diner that on any other day would have been busy and filled with students. Their English was limited—they were Romanian immigrants and had helped the estate owners for almost four decades. They'd brought along photographs to show me. I spent too many hours nodding and smiling and wishing I had the sort of companionship they possessed together. I was thankful for many things, including the chance to be alone when the day was done.

I hadn't told Jesse that I was coming to the city because I hadn't known in advance that Stuart would make a trip out of town, and when I did know, I thought I would be a surprise guest at Jesse's benefit fundraiser. The train was late arriving in the city; a rain storm was backing up traffic. The walk to the theater was slow, darting between and around pedestrians, tourists, cyclists, and umbrellas. I was grateful the weather was so lousy; the rain kept me focused on my path and not revisiting memories.

There was a small crowd outside the building when I reached the theater, and I looked for someone I might know, but I didn't see anyone and didn't really want to be seen. I didn't want to have to explain my absence, my choices, my new life to someone who might frown and respond, "but you must miss the city."

The theater entrance was beside a pizzeria, a doorway that led up a narrow flight of stairs to a dark room with risers and benches. I took a program from an usher and sat near the back of the room. It was full of Jesse's doodlelings and lists, but I noticed that there was no mention of Pussy Couture performing in the workshop.

Before I had a chance to study the program further, the audience lights dimmed and the spotlights brightened on a stage with two empty chairs. Jesse was standing in a long-sleeved white business shirt and black slacks and wearing a paisley neck tie; behind him was a young man dressed in a white T-shirt, khaki shorts, and black ankle high work boots.

Jesse began reciting one of his lists, a rant against consumerism, capitalism, corporations, and white-collar greed. His whining delivery elicited snickers and connected him to his audience. His monologue alternated with a list recited by the young man behind him. His list was one of names and ages. "Mitch, 33; Wade, 36; Frank, 38; Jack, 28;" and it sent the audience into a hush.

Jesse began taking off his tie, then his shirt and pants, and his lists changed. "I hated sports. I loved jocks. I went to the gym to find a chest and when I couldn't get the one I wanted I decided I would build one of my own." The young man began to take off his T-shirt, now reciting a list of addresses and buildings. "Sutton Place, 2D. Sauna, West 4th Street. Alleyway, Houston." The young man had a beautiful physique.

Jesse angled himself so he faced the young man. An argument began:

"You gave up! You gave up on all of us."

"I needed to change."

"You ran away."

"I was burned out."

I realized why Jesse had stopped talking to me about Pussy's behavior at rehearsals—he must have fired her or aggravated her enough to make her quit. And the lists were too familiar. They were mine. Lists I had read to Jesse over the phone. Jesse had stolen my words and ideas. The play evolved into a theme of who was right? Who was wrong?

I held in my shock, floating through thoughts of anger and denial and disbelief over what Jesse was presenting on stage.

I had intended to surprise Jesse after the show—the next day was his birthday and I had been prepared to stay overnight on his couch, but I was in shock, and angry, and I put on my jacket, slipped on my backpack, and opened the umbrella and went back out into the rain. As I walked away, I argued in my mind with Jesse, an argument I doubted that I would follow through on with him the next time we spoke. He had stolen my story, stolen my voice. He had staged our conversations and arguments.

I felt too alienated and dispirited to remain in the city and I wandered into the bus station and found the next bus that could get me close to the college.

I wanted a cigarette. I wanted a beer or a twist of bourbon. But I knew that the urge would send me into depression and a hangover. It was a long bus ride, traveling through areas I wasn't familiar with. The sky grew dim and darker and the view became reflections of lights.

The rain had stopped when I reached the college town, though a damp uneasiness remained. The drive back to the cottage passed by the grocery store, and I decided to pick up some last-minute items before crashing for the night.

I entered the store and grabbed a hand-held basket, found milk and chips, and was headed into the soda aisle when two men pushing a shopping cart rounded the corner and stopped in front of me to avoid a collision. One of them was Stuart. The shock registered on both of our faces, but at the moment I didn't think anything was amiss—I was glad to see him and was smiling—and assumed that he had been trying to reach me but we hadn't connected yet because I had been in the city.

"You're back!" I said. "When did you get back?"

My expression was of surprise and joy. I realized he was flushing red, floundering for breath, his eyes nervously darting, and that his hand was shaking. The man standing beside him was similar to Stuart's appearance: age, eyeglasses, tall, stiff posture. "This is Hal," Stuart said. "Hal came to visit."

They looked like brothers. No; they looked like lovers. Partners. Two men who had molded themselves after each other. I realized that Stuart had lied to me. He had never left town to visit his parents; he had been spending the week with Hal— here.

I smiled and moved around him and tried to start shopping in another aisle. My heart was beating too fast and my face was red, trying not to feel like I was caught in the scene of a bad soap opera.

A moment later Stuart appeared alone. "It's not what it looks like," he said.

"Of course, it isn't," I answered. "I know who he is, and he hasn't a clue who I am."

"We had always planned it, before I met you. He brought me some of my furniture."

When I had no answer for him, he added, "We're not sleeping together. It's over between us. He's just here as my friend."

I wanted to believe him, but I couldn't hear the honesty in his voice. "I can't leave him alone to see you while he's here," Stuart said. "Please be patient. We've been together for a long time, so I can't mistreat him. I'll find a way to make this up to you."

It is hard to tell a story with grief as a main character. There are urges to outline its stages: denial, anger, bargaining, depression, and acceptance. There is a tendency to heighten details for empathy. Grief is as deeply personal as love and pain; I was grieving both for the life I'd lost as much as the one I'd been unable to find. When I lived in the city, it was always easy to find a free copy of a current magazine or the day's newspaper. On the subway, at a desk, or in a library or a bookstore, I would read the obituaries. It wasn't difficult to fill in any blanks. I recognized that death was not going to disappear; I knew that other gay men were going through these same experiences. Still, every step I wanted to take forward—to accept and change and begin anew—seemed thwarted.

I learned of Peter's death in the daily newspaper that was delivered to the architect's office. Peter, a former boyfriend, was an actor I had met the first year I lived in Manhattan. He was eight years my elder, already in a relationship with a prominent theater director, a man two decades older than himself. Although I possessed that youthful desire to be an actor, I also had a self-awareness that I had a limited talent that relied more on age and looks. I knew I had a writer's voice in my head, though I didn't understand how to express it or even if I had a story to tell. By the time I had settled into Manhattan, Peter had a reputation as a notable performer, with a string of memorable off-Broadway roles and a Broadway debut. He had the classic features of a Greek hero: a tall, strong physique, a warrior's long nose and a solid chin, a helmet of soft, curly brown hair that flowed from his scalp as if it were streams from a fountain. He was teaching a weekend acting workshop in the West Village, not far from where I was living at the time, and I enrolled in his class, hoping I might conquer my fear of auditions and find more confidence in myself, but also hoping in two parts: that someone might discover something in me, and that I might discover something about myself that would help me to become a writer.

The first class concentrated on warm-up techniques, preparing the voice and body, finding relaxation, and focusing the mind, which to me was a showy way of doing throat clearings, limb stretching, and chanting. It was a humorless class; everyone was too serious about their techniques. I was the only student in jeans and a T-shirt; the others had used a small locker room to change into somber black and gray dance clothes.

Peter spent time with each student, using the palms of his hands to flatten backs and stomachs and arch necks and spines. I couldn't help but smile and laugh because I felt silly trying to take deep breaths and contort my body into unnatural positions. He asked me to stay after class and, as I waited while the other students peppered him with questions, rubbing away the sweat and dirt with the edges of my T-shirt, I felt he would encourage me to drop out and abandon the theater. Instead, he asked me where I was from, how long I had been in the city, and if I had studied elsewhere.

He asked if I had more comfortable clothes to practice and rehearse in, and if I preferred a jockstrap or a dance belt. My astonished expression provided him with an answer I couldn't make. "I'm sure I've got something you can borrow," he said and looked at his watch. "I've got a dinner appointment, but why don't you walk with me back to my apartment and we can find something for you to use for the next class."

On the walk from the Village to his apartment in Chelsea, he talked about living in the city, the history of the buildings, the shows he had seen, what actors and playwrights and celebrities lived on the blocks we passed. No one had ever educated— or talked—to me like this. I'd spent my college years studying the comings and goings of the bohemians of Greenwich Village, reading the Arts and Leisure section of the Sunday *Times* every week in the college library, and memorizing the facts and dates noted in the annual editions of *Theater World* I had discovered in the stacks of the campus library, so I enthusiastically attempted to match him with as many details as I could remember.

Peter lived in a four-story brownstone he shared with the director, with rooms full of books and props and antiques acquired from years of experience and travel. While I was naïve about a lot of things, I wasn't clueless as to Peter's intentions that day. I followed him into the bedroom he shared with the director, who was conveniently rehearsing a show out of town, where Peter opened a top drawer of a bureau, pulled out a handful of jocks and thongs and dance belts and tossed them onto the bed. "You might want to try them on, make sure one fits," he said.

Before I had a chance to unbutton the top button of my jeans, Peter's hands were already there. Our affair lasted through the six weeks of classes, after which the director returned to town and Peter began rehearsals for a new play, but we continued to get together sporadically and spontaneously over the next eight years—either at the townhouse or my apartment. Peter had many affairs and never experienced any guilt over any of them; his director-partner even encouraged them. Peter's favorite maxim onstage and off—never be ashamed—was something he taught me our first afternoon together. I saw him off and on until he fell ill during the rehearsals of another play and withdrew from the production. I called him many times when I heard that news, and for months he avoided me because, oddly, he felt ashamed that he was ill—till the day I left a lengthy message telling him about Mitch's death, and that I thought I would be leaving Manhattan soon.

I knew I couldn't handle Peter's illness after witnessing Mitch's decline and avoiding Wade's. In many ways I felt ashamed about leaving him behind when I left Manhattan. But Peter had the director and his friends and resources to help him survive, And die. What I regretted was that I never had with Peter what he had with the director and I used that fact to ease my guilt.

I handled the news of Peter's death with a quiet stoicism, refusing to break down in tears, unlike the way I had handled the losses of both Wade and Mitch. I took long bike rides through the cold, bleak November landscapes to clear my mind and help me avoid reaching for a cigarette or a drink. I thought I had accepted that death was now part of my landscape, accepted Peter's passing, along with those of Mitch and Wade and many others I knew; thought that I was finally handling grief like an adult should, when the news of Eric's death came. I knew Eric from college; he had been my first love. My secret love. We had shared everything with each other but had not let anyone else know of it. His obituary was a small line of type in a digest of news in my college alumni magazine that found its way to the mailbox outside the cottage. Eric had been living in Orlando, working as an ambulance driver. I had wanted to tell him about my working on the convention hotel project that was under construction near where he lived. I thought about him every time I couriered another package or tube of architectural blueprints south. I knew from another college friend that he had not given up his spontaneous partying. It had been one of things I loved most about him, and the one I knew I needed to escape.

As each morning arrived, I woke hoping something in me would change, that the person I was would become someone else, but only the weather grew fierce and cold, and I chose warmer clothes to wear as if to protect myself from sorrow. In the evenings the campus glowed in the amber light of sunsets. Maggie's mood brightened as the heat in our workspace lessened for a few days. She giggled as she talked of Luke's high school homework—"He asked me a Calculus question last night," Maggie said. "I haven't even used Algebra since I was in school. I told him to ask me a question about Probability. He said they don't get to that until next semester."

"The cops confiscated my AZT," Jesse said when I answered the phone. "I should file a lawsuit."

I could hear the agitation in his voice. He sounded winded, as if he'd just lost an argument.

I hadn't spoken to him in more than a week—I had a lot of built-up animosity that I didn't want to dump on him. "Back up," I said and turned off the television. It was late and I was trying to unwind before heading to bed, using the TV as background noise as I jotted down some thoughts for a new story. "Start at the beginning. Why were you arrested?"

"Are you living in a vacuum?" he said. Now his tone was annoyed. "Is your head buried in the ground? Stop the Church! We were protesting the church and the Cardinal. Why have you suddenly turned into a Middle American idiot? I walked into the cathedral and they carried me out in a stretcher."

Jesse segued into a monologue about being charged with four counts, including resisting arrest, because the Cardinal refused to allow condoms and safer-sex education materials to be distributed at hospitals, hospices, and shelters. "His morality can go to hell."

When he took a breath, I asked, "Jesse, why are you battling the Cardinal and Catholic church? Why is this so important to you?"

"It's the principal. The abuse of power."

"But you don't use condoms."

I felt his anger in his silence. "That's my choice," he said. "That's my right. I'm honest with my partners."

I remained quiet; I wasn't going to point out his own recklessness or that someone else might consider him a hypocrite. Then, after another pause, as if he understood that I was not going pacify him, he said, "I'm sorry about Peter." When I didn't respond, he added, in his annoyed voice, "I'm sorry you didn't come and talk to me after my performance. My feelings were hurt, you know."

I was silent, trying to gather my opinions and emotions. "You stole my story," I answered. It was no longer a yell, or a shout out loud, or an argument in my head, but a whispered fact.

There was another beat of silence as Jesse thought about my statement. "I told my version of your story," he said. "Which is my story to tell."

"I'm not as upset as I was."

"Don't make me apologize for your life," he said. Then, to soften his stance, he added, "because you are a part of my life."

In that moment, I realized Jesse was different. I didn't hate him the way I hated Mitch. I enjoyed our war. I enjoyed Jesse attempting to keep me honest and vice versa.

"How was the feedback?" I asked. "Were there any reviews?"

"It was a humbling and dishonest experience," Jesse added. "I want to blame it on a certain drag queen, but I know I'm a prick, too. I'd rather write my messy, bitter anecdotes in solitude for applause. So I am putting all the blame on you. And your story."

"I guess I should be grateful for the recognition."

"You're a wonderful writer," he said. "But not what my audience expects of me."

"Thanks, I guess."

"I turned in my manuscript," he added. "They want to call my mess a novel."

"That's wonderful. Congratulations."

"I'm scheduled to go into the hospital for a blood transfusion next week," he said.

"Do you have someone to go with you?"

"I do," he said. "No need to feel guilty."

"Jesse, if you need me, I will help you."

"That's the final act," he said. "We're still at intermission."


A few days before Christmas, Greg and his wife threw a holiday party at their home, inviting his team of architects and draftsmen and interns and much of the staff who worked for the more famous brand-name one. They lived four blocks away from the office, in a small house that was built at the end of World War II and which had been enlarged and expanded until it had become a mini-mansion. The moment I stepped inside and saw the candles and decorated trees and wreaths and accent pillows, I knew the event was designed to be a showcase for Colleen's interior design skills. The house looked like it was set to be photographed for a magazine and everyone had that sort of frightened look like they were worried they might spill or drop something and spoil the picture.

It was a stiff affair, the lights too bright, the eggnog spikeless, the guests forming little cliques of conversations that modeled the cliques at the office. The coworkers who never spoke to me at work made no effort to converse with me at the party. The famous brand-name architect and his girlfriend, also an architect, made a brief guest appearance, and the room where he held court swelled with the glare of attention and its seekers.

I roamed through the corners of the house, trying not to look as if I was snooping. I was unhappy to be alone and single at the party, still smarting from Stuart's absence and worrying how to put an end to our relationship, and if it was any kind of "relationship" at all. I stopped at every bookshelf I passed in the house, reading the titles, hoping to erase my anger about Stuart's lying. Most of the books were focused on design and photography and rather meaningless to me, but I found a children's book misplaced on a shelf, and it made me smile, as if I had discovered the hidden golden egg in the illustration of a forest. I thumbed through the pages in an attempt not to feel awkward, not to leave the room and step outside and pretend to smoke a cigarette and think of all those inside as fools. Maggie had brought along Luke and was proudly introducing her stepson to everyone as if he were her new boyfriend, tucking her arm through his as if he were a brightly colored balloon that would float away at any minute. Everyone was dressed a bit more formally than the daily office attire of business casual, except for myself; I had discarded most of my party attire when I left the city. Maggie had pulled her hair tightly back from her face; she wore a red embroidered bolero jacket over a light green blouse and skirt. She looked elegant and brittle, with a glazed look in her eyes, different from the more usual one I saw in our tower of horror, as if she were full of happy indifference. Her vibes had changed too. I could tell she was in love, a defiant love, a love she wasn't supposed to have, and at the time I thought she must have resumed the affair with her astrologist friend in Baltimore and this was the reason why Bryan was absent and had not joined her at the party. She was using

Luke as a decoy to avoid the truth of her crumbling marriage. I had a short conversation with Luke about a baseball movie I had seen and thought he might enjoy before I drifted into a conversation with Keith and his wife Rachel. They were both dressed as if they were headed to church to listen to a sermon. She was petite and wide-mouthed, clutching her purse with both hands. There wasn't a curl in her hair—it was thin and dark and straight, as if it had been glued to her skull. She tipped her dark head and big eyes upward, stretching out her neck and chin, aloof and annoyed, as if she were not drawing enough attention, looking up and over us to find a better conversation until Keith asked for recommendations of Broadway shows; they were headed into the city for the holidays, and I struggled to avoid repeating Stuart's noxious opinions as those of my own. But a small argument suddenly arose between the couple when Rachel complained that there was not enough food at the party and they would need to leave soon to find a more suitable dinner, and Keith reminded her that he was trying to cut down on calorie consumption and lose weight.

Rachel threw me a look and said, "It's a lousy time of year to go on a diet, right?"

I caught Keith's reaction and it dawned on me that he was not happy in his marriage, or at least in this moment he wasn't happy. I looked at my watch and said I needed to leave. As I was retrieving my coat from the small bedroom where I had left it with those of the other guests, Greg appeared in the doorway, blocking my exit. I could tell he was summing me up, wondering what it would be like if we got together—I'd seen that sort of hungry look in a man before. I tried to be oblivious of it, thanking him for asking me to the party, telling him to thank his wife for me. I reached the doorway and stopped, waiting for him to break his stance and let me leave. But he held firm, as if it were his silent way of communicating his desire, so I held his gaze, challenging him to make a first move. I saw the twitch in his lip. I saw the shift in his eyes. But nothing else happened. We were interrupted by the plodding steps of Alan, the pale-faced office manager, approaching to retrieve his own coat.

If Jesse were to tell my story, he would write that I ran away at an early age. That I abandoned my family, my friends, my girlfriends and boyfriends in my hometown because I was small-minded with big dreams and I didn't want to face up to any responsibility. He would be unmerciful, saying I was egotistical from birth, jealous of my older brother's freedom, resentful of my parents' focus on my younger sister.

There would be some truth to Jesse's version, but it would be Jesse's truth, not my own.

This is not a story about my family, of feeling different, of moving away because of ambition or to find freedom. I'm not out to disparage my family, only to say that my differences from them were part of my decision to live elsewhere. I did not disown my family; to me that was unthinkable—though even at a distance they often caused me anxiety and regret. Some years I simply told my parents I was not traveling to visit them—there were costs, there were commitments elsewhere, there was a desire to be anywhere except adrift alone in a sea of indifferent siblings, spouses, and their children.

I had come out to my parents on my thirtieth birthday, telling them in a phone call about a friend I knew who worked as a stage manager who had died and why I went to his funeral. I went to his funeral because we had dated briefly the first year I lived in the city. I used the term "date" symbolically to emphasize the coming out objective to my parents, sparing them the details of the two-day tryst I had had with the stage manager at his uptown apartment. Their response was polite, directed to knowing more details of my friend who had died and to offer their condolences. They did not inquire about my health, though my mother sighed and whispered, "Darling, I hope you are careful." On my next trip to visit my parents, my mother said that only the immediate family knew about "the choices" I had made. Before I had a chance to correct her that it was never a "choice," she added, "We don't think anyone else needs to know this outside of the family," confirming what I already knew about my parents. It was a fact they were ashamed to admit they had a son who was gay.

That winter I found no excuse not to visit—I had a silly notion that it could be restorative, in the same way that moving to the college town was intended to be, that removing myself from any kind of comfort situation, I would peel back my resistances and understand the real person I was and wanted to become. I drove many hours, fretting about my life and my job, and worrying about the upcoming maintenance costs for my car, how I could disentangle myself from Stuart with the least amount of drama, and potential scenarios to consider if Jesse required help.

My old bedroom had been turned into my mother's craft room where she made flower arrangements for the church. I slept in my sister's former bedroom. My sister and her husband slept downstairs in the living room on a pull-out couch. She'd given birth to a son earlier in the year and there were bags and bottles and make-shift diaper stations. As I held and cooed at my new nephew, my sister worried about money and exhaustion. Her husband watched the TV and took smoking breaks. No one asked if I was depressed, or noticed that I was.

My mother was glad of my decision to leave New York City. "I wish you'd move closer to home though," she added. "So I don't have to worry about you so much." She led me upstairs to the walk-in closet in her bedroom. "The important papers are up there, in that box," she said and pointed to a shelf.

"Is there something I should know?" I asked, suddenly alarmed that my mother or my father might be ill.

"Your Daddy wants us to travel more," she said. "We want you to know where the important papers are."

I took breaks to drive to the grocery store or run errands. I drove by my high school friend Andy's house. It had been repainted a darker shade of off-white and looked smaller; the basketball hoop was gone. My father had told me his younger brother had committed suicide and I stared at the house and wondered about causes and scenarios. My mother mentioned a neighbor who had gone to our church had died. I avoided mentioning

Peter's death, or Frank's, or Eric's, or any details of Mitch and Wade; I shielded my grief and concerns through family gatherings and dinner. The house next door was vacant. My father mentioned that my high school girlfriend's house had been sold to a "mixed family." I thought of life happening without me, things going on, some things remaining, other things changing.

I left my family grateful that my unreliable secondhand car was able to survive the return road trip, though somewhere near the state border the car began to rumble and chug and I knew its days were limited.

In many ways, returning to see my family for the holidays made me more determined to return to the college town and try to make things work in my life. I didn't want to put my life on pause again; I wanted to get on with it.

In January, Alan, the office manager, arrived one morning at our perch. Maggie gave him the cold shoulder or, rather, a withering stare because it was so hot in our office alcove, which didn't surprise me, because he hadn't climbed upstairs to speak with her. He looked down at me sitting on my stool and said, "Greg mentioned you're usually late. You know you should make an effort to be here on time."

"Late?" I echoed back. "Greg said this?"

Alan didn't respond, only tightened his lips as if to emphasize the point. I distinctly disliked that I had been the subject of a private conversation, or worse, that Greg had spent his mornings watching the parking lot to see when I arrived because he didn't have a better view. I knew at that moment I was going to leave this job, but I wasn't sure yet how or when because I needed the income to survive.

"Greg would like to see you here on time," Alan finally said. "We'll have to adjust your salary if you continue to be late."

"Then you'll pay me overtime when I stay late to get the packages out the door, correct?"

My comment seemed to take him by surprise. "Let's make an effort to keep regular office hours," he said and left.

I seethed and stewed. Maggie avoided me, twisting and lifting her hair off her neck and scribbling in her journal. She was busy with her own dark clouds. Greg arrived at my desk sometime after lunch, with an armful of drawings to be sent to Florida. I glared at him with mounting anger, until I said, with acerbic glee, "I hope I can get all of this done during my standard workday hours. Otherwise, I will need to put in for overtime pay if

I stay late to finish any of this. It's against the law if you don't pay hourly employees overtime wages."

He tilted his head, as if he were imitating his wife, gave me an astonished smirk as if I had just lit his surfboard on fire and tossed it out to sea, and disappeared.

As it happened, I was late the next day because of car trouble, and the following day as well. As I was climbing the stairs into the heat of the hellish attic, I was trying to calculate if I could survive on unemployment pay if I were fired. But if anyone was keeping watch over my hours, they didn't appear at my desk with times and numbers; only Keith made an appearance in the afternoon with more drawings to be put in the mail. He'd lost weight since the holidays, working out on a treadmill he had purchased and quickly abandoned because the noise and vibrations in his apartment had so annoyed his wife that he had started running mornings at the campus gym.

"No biking today, I guess?" he said in a lighthearted manner, as he handed over a set of drawings. Because of the cold weather I hadn't been biking since before the holidays, and I gave him a weak smile when he added, "You should leave early, before it starts snowing."

I wanted to tell him that arriving late and leaving early would only make my job performance look worse, and the truth of the matter was, I only wanted to be as good an employee as the office space my employer provided me to work in.

I was determined to make it to work on time the following day, however, despite the snowfall, but once again my car defeated me. In the morning when I set out to leave for work, the car engine wouldn't turn over. Nothing. Not a sound. I wasn't even sure if the battery could be jump-started. I went back inside the cottage and left a message for Alan that I would not be at work.

I should probably add now that money has been an issue all of my life, the lack of it, not so much the pursuit of it. I'd been working since I was fifteen, not that unusual really, but my debt never seemed to go away, and I lived paycheck to paycheck. I wasn't a reckless shopaholic. I didn't take exorbitant vacations. I didn't gamble or invest and suffer market crashes (because I had no savings), so I had no vices to explain my constant tread along the national poverty line in spite of, or perhaps because of, a college education. In recent years my only extravagance had been to pay for Mitch's medicines and groceries and rent when his own income stopped, but three months of that had been enough to pitch me into a deep credit crisis I was still trying to recover from.

So that snowy morning I went back to my bed and lay down and worried, until I willed myself up around lunchtime, telling myself it was time to grow up, be a man and an adult, and move ahead with my life. I couldn't afford the cost of having the car towed to a garage. The storm had passed and outside the sunlight was blinding against the new-fallen snow, but from my window it looked as if the main roadway had been cleared; traffic was moving even if it was moving slowly. I put on a pair of sneakers—I was too poor and stubborn to buy snow boots—and walked around the side of the cottage and looked up the hill I had biked along many times. I had never sought Rick and his wife for help before, but I needed to now, my shoes soaking wet when I reached their farmhouse.

Rick came to the door and waved me inside looking older and more frail than I had expected, but I didn't have the energy to act out pleasant small talk, so I hastily explained that I was having trouble with my car and did he have anything to help me jump-start the battery? I was always unclear how well he spoke or understood English, but I was grateful he was a no-nonsense man, and he could tell I had showed up at his door because I needed his help. He put on a coat and hat and I followed him across a long yard to a shed where he unlocked the door and pulled on a chain light. The shed wasn't big enough for two people, so I stood outside, stamping my feet against the snow as I waited. Despite my desire to be in a relationship, I had always prided myself on my independence, trying to make a go of it without involving others, so I hated having to ask for help, hated feeling grateful, hated feeling like I would have to someday return a favor. But at the same time, I wanted to hug him and thank him for being alive and at home and willing and able to help me out of this mess.

Rick found jumper cables and a battery that looked older than my car. An hour later, after some unsuccessful zaps and pings and a smoking break (his), he had gotten my car started and I drove him back up the hillside to his cottage.

I won't elaborate on the humiliation of the remainder of the day, except to say that the snow did not prevent any of the car salesmen from showing up at to the automobile dealerships at the fringes of the suburbs. My car had no trade-in value, but it did contribute to the ease with which a lease on a new car could be arranged. I knew I was at a disadvantage and was being overcharged, but I needed a way forward, so I nodded and initialed and signed on every dotted line.

I'd like to believe that I was brave and adventurous and determined to succeed when I moved to New York. I was twenty-three and had only been to the city a handful of times; by the late 1970s, the dream of being a part of the professional theater meant facing the challenges of Times Square—the noise and the traffic, the brusqueness and uncertainty of every step. 42nd Street was a carnival of X-rated cinemas, street hustlers, drug dealers, and adult bookstores. It could be exciting, but it could also be a risk. I arrived alone, found a place to live, and discovered the streets and shops and subway lines I needed to use to survive. I arrived with a knapsack, a portable typewriter, a hefty college tuition debt, and no savings. I was a fool with a dream. I had no friends in the city to rely on. No one supported my move—my parents were worried and displeased. My hometown friends were aghast. My college friends placed bets that I wouldn't last long.

It was a late summer evening, a few weeks after I had moved to Manhattan—I'd just finished seeing a free concert in Central Park and was making my way back to my apartment in the West Village. I was trying to save money, so I was walking on 42nd street from Grand Central to Times Square, cautious of everyone around me—the street was dark and empty with pockets of lights and shadows and there was always a concern of the crime around the borders of Times Square. After I passed Sixth Avenue there was a building with large concrete planters framing a small plaza outside a skyscraper. I noticed a tallish man moving past the planters—he seemed to be saying something to three shorter men who I noticed were hidden in the shadows. As I made my way closer—to pass them—I could see that the tall man had stepped away and was waiting to jaywalk to the north side of the street. As I passed by a concrete planter, a short man grabbed at my pants' back pocket, ripped the fabric, and stole my wallet. Another guy clipped the knapsack from my shoulder. I was about to yell out, when a third guy took a punch at my face as I stepped away, and I stumbled to the sidewalk and saw the three short men—or boys—running away as I yelled, "Stop!"

The tall man came to my side and helped me to my feet. He was thin and had headful of wiry black curls and a thick stubble of dark beard. He was wearing designer jeans and an expensive dress shirt with a wide collar. I thanked him—I thought his presence had scared off the robbers and saved me more harm. I said I was okay, but I was distraught because my wallet and knapsack were gone. I looked around, suspicious of other possible assailants. The tall man mentioned that there was a police station at Times Square and he would go with me to report the robbery.

The tall man stood beside me as I spoke to a policeman. Afterward, he introduced himself and asked if I needed assistance to get home. Were my keys stolen? he asked. Did I need subway fare to get home?

The keys were still in my pocket, but I didn't tell the man that my wallet had no money in it. I was down to my last subway token until I could cash a paycheck the following day. I worried how to repair my jeans—I didn't have enough money to buy another pair. The man suggested we walk to a diner that was a few blocks away. "I bet you could use a meal and a drink," he said. "My treat."

At the diner the man talked about himself. He handed me his business card and said he was a journalist—he had been to the same performance I saw that night in Central Park. He wrote down my phone number on a small slip of the receipt. He gave me enough money for a cab down to the Village. The next morning he called me. "This is Mitch," the man said. "We met last night."

I've replayed this scene in my mind for many years, searching for details, forgotten clues. At one point I wondered what alignment the planets and stars were in for our lives to cross at this moment. I've always considered that Mitch saved me that night, distracted me from my misery long enough to laugh, and in doing so, made it impossible for me to walk away from him.

I can't remember who told me that all it takes sometimes is one small, good thing to turn around a string of bad luck, but a new set of reliable albeit expensive wheels didn't seem to apply. When I returned to work, I found my workspace crammed with drawings to mail out. Maggie was unenthusiastic when I explained I had gotten a new car, because she was annoyed with having to cover for me while I was absent, so it was a slow, daunting morning that ended when Alan appeared and said, "Let's start over. How about joining me for lunch?"

We wrapped ourselves in coats and walked to the small deli near the edge of campus, where I learned that Alan lived with his partner, Martin, in an apartment complex on the other side of the Interstate. Alan was a few years older than I was and had a cherubic face that made it difficult to take him seriously. Before joining the architectural firm, he had been in the human relations department of a pharmaceutical company, where it became clear to him that there was no career track for him to pursue. His partner, Martin, had been a high school English and Drama teacher until he left to become the managing director of a nearby regional theater. I was curious about his partner's theater background and why he had left it behind—Alan hinted that the theater wanted to take a "new direction," which I understood to mean it was either having financial issues or had produced a string of bombs. I mentioned my own work in the theater in New York, name-dropped a few actors and directors, including Peter and his director-partner, and when Alan asked why I had left the city behind, knowing already what my likely answer would be, I remained vague myself, simply answering, "It was time for a change." I didn't want to let my employer know that I was having a breakdown, though it was obvious most days, but I did mention to Alan that I had been dating someone locally but was uncertain if it would continue—Stuart had phoned me a few days before to say that he hoped we might get together soon. At lunch, nothing was said about my job performance, or my late comings and early goings, or of the lack of a decent work environment, but this was the moment that I began to think of Alan as more of an advocate and ally than as another foolish bureaucratic antagonist.

This is not a story about Stuart, his *carpe diem* attitude and Latin mottos, or my relationship with him, or lack of one, but he was instrumental in my awakening, anger breathing in a new ability to stand up for myself, to play a part in navigating my own uncharted path. All I expected was for him to tell the truth and for me to trust him, and though I felt we both fell short, I still embraced him when he found his way back to my cottage and bedroom. I used him as much as he used me. But because he had lied to me once, I was suspicious of everything he said and felt the need to prod deeper into his statements and opinions with questions until a grim speck of reality surfaced. And in the process, I learned that Stuart was not a man that I liked.

But the sex was too addictive to step away from. I should spend a moment explaining some aspects of my sex life. Though I was HIV-negative, in the early years of my sexual awakening I had experienced an array of STDs and I'd come to worry that I was easily prone to infections.

Since Stuart's return from Boston and his persistence to get together, our bedroom time had ended in arguments with neither of us satisfied. To him I was "stingy" and "withholding." To me he was "uncaring" and "reckless."

I might have eased myself into submission if it hadn't been for a conversation a few days later when

Stuart casually let it slip that he had been to see a doctor. "Ray, one of my graduate students, tested positive," he said. "So I thought it was time to be tested again, too."

Question by question I was able to extract an admission that Stuart had slept with the student in early fall, before we met. I didn't ask for the details of who was the passive or active partner, if it had been once or several times, or why the student felt it was important to disclose his status now to Stuart, because I felt the facts could only anger me. But I knew I wasn't happy in what was becoming for me a codependent scenario. My new confidence seemed crushed, and that led to thoughts that perhaps all the men I had dated were not at fault—I was the one who was unwilling to maintain a relationship.

But a bigger issue soon surfaced and, once again, it was related to sex: Stuart and I were eating at a Mexican restaurant. We were both in good moods, though tired from work. I had never interrogated Stuart about Hal, and Stuart had not offered much explanation, but our own relationship included the mutual admiration of other men who happened to catch our attention, whether watching television, or in this case, eating at a restaurant. When we were together we would often comment on the fellow, admiring him as "handsome," "sexy," "intriguing" or "stunning" and sometimes commenting on a characteristic the man displayed, like a handsome face, dreamy eyes, nice arms, or great ass. I didn't find this practice as distressing with Stuart as I have sometimes felt with other guys, particularly, because I thought I had Stuart's sexual attention.

During our dinner conversation, Stuart remarked on the beauty of a young man sitting nearby, and I agreed and then said in a lighthearted manner that it was all right for him to "look" but not "touch."

Stuart's reaction was swift and hard. "I don't believe in monogamy," he said.

I had never discussed the issue of monogamy with a partner, in truth, because I had never reached that point, but I did feel that for myself, if I was developing an attachment for a guy—on the path of falling in love—I didn't want to be sleeping with someone else. I knew serial monogamy was seldom the route for gay men, but it was still what I desired, even if I felt it might be unattainable for both my partner and myself.

"So you're still sleeping with Hal," I said, more of a statement than a question.

Stuart hesitated a moment and then said, "Yes."

It was confirmation that he had lied to me before. "And your student?" I asked.

He didn't answer, but looked away from me, so I knew that this was also the truth. I felt like a fool but remained calm and silent through the remainder of the dinner. I realized at that moment monogamy was never the issue. It was honesty. If Stuart had lied to be about one thing, he could lie about another. When we reached the cottage, I told Stuart that it was best that we be apart that evening. He looked at me with a hurt expression and his eyes pooled with tears. "Don't do this to me now," he said.

"To you?" I answered. "What am I doing to you?"

It was a miserable month. The weather went from snowy to freezing rain—even with the new car the commute to work was frustrating. Giving up Stuart was like stopping smoking, a few steps forward, a few steps back. I did not believe I could trust him and thought I would be the one who was hurt. We met a couple of times for make-up and break-up sex. The afternoon I reached him during his office hours at the college and offered to drop off the clothes, toiletries, and record albums he had kept at the cottage, he grew angry. "Why are you doing this over the phone?"

"We can't keep doing this," I answered.

"But you've been there for me," he said.

"For sex. You call me for sex. You show up for sex."

"But we're friends too. We've done other things. Can't we find a way to work this out?"

"I'm not looking for a sex buddy," I said.

"Can't we be open? Can't we see others? I don't want to rush into this."

"Because you're still in another relationship."

"I still have feelings for Hal."

"And Ray?"

"Why are you doing this by phone?"

"Because you know I don't have the will power to do it in person. You would start crying and we would end up having sex again."

"Is that so bad?"

"I need a break from this," I said and hung up.

I put everything into a plastic shopping bag and left it on the front door handle of his apartment, but I didn't have the confidence that I was doing the right thing. Mitch would have called me foolish for expecting a gay man to be monogamous.

Late that night, I kept thinking I was wrong for calling an end to it, till I reminded myself that it was more than an issue of monogamy. Stuart had been lying to me. I couldn't trust him. I stood outside the cottage in the cold night air, looking up at the sky, at the stars or the swiftly moving clouds, and again wondered why I had ended up here of all places in the world.

Miles away in Manhattan, Jesse complained about the cold, but used excuses about editing his manuscript to miss demonstrations and meetings. He phoned me after every call with his editor—there were questions from the publisher's legal team, there was canvassing for blurbs, there was an argument with a copyeditor over a suggested word change, and a request for a better author's photo, all of which sent Jesse into a tailspin. Somewhere in these calls, I told Jesse some good news had turned up: my story about shopping for a winter coat had been accepted by a literary magazine at one of colleges that had rejected me as a graduate student. "Of course they want to publish it," Jesse said. "You're terrific! I taught you everything. Where would you be without me?"

Maggie's birthday arrived, a cake appeared in our workspace, and I had to vacate the area because the heat and noise were unbearable. Maggie's energy seemed changed—she was quieter, more introspective. She seldom wore her hair down; it was always tied up into a knot or braided into bun. Instead of drawing me into conversations, she now sat at her desk, studying the cards of the Tarot deck that she kept hidden beneath a paper tray. One morning, she arrived at our workspace

and scribbled something in her journal and handed
it to me to read:

*my body is not a demon*
*life is not random*
*accidental desire*
*mistakes with aftershocks*

I smiled and asked her if she was pregnant.

"I don't deserve it," she said.

"What do you mean?"

"You wouldn't understand."

"How do you know?"

"You'd only side against me."

"I'm on your side. I've always been on your side."

She looked at me as if I were mad, though this
time I wasn't. I was stronger. She patted the clip at
the back of her neck that held her hair into place.
"I'm not ready to talk about it yet," she said. Her
eyes were large and watery, as if they would spill
with tears.

I didn't press her further because I felt I knew
the story. Her Baltimore astrologist must be the
father and her dilemma was that she had not told
anyone this news. Instead of dwelling on her issues,
I had begun to think about the next stage of my life.
Stuart had stopped calling. I had no desire to answer
ads to meet other guys. Instead, I began to write
small anecdotes about my life, each where I learned
something about myself—forever the student—how

I stopped smoking, why I enjoyed biking—to me as self-revelatory as Maggie's tremors. I thought I could string them together into a story. Find my way into writing a memoir or a thinly disguised novel.

My life might have been all right if not for the fact that late one Friday night, or rather, early one Saturday morning, there was a loud series of knocks at the cottage door. My first thought was that it was Stuart wanting to make amends and have sex and spend the night and that I should ignore it, but my next worry was that it could be the Rick needing to take his wife to the hospital for an emergency. When I opened the door, I saw it was Keith. He was drunk and mumbling about not wanting to drive back to his house and asking if he could crash on my couch until morning.

I let him inside, worried about his condition and my clutter in the room, moving a pile of books and newspapers and finding him a blanket. I asked him where Rachel was and he said he had left her.

"What do you mean?" I asked him. "Do you want me to call her? Won't she be worried?"

He looked at me with his large eyes and said, "Mistake..." and then in an annoyed tone, added, "Haven't you ever made a mistake?"

I gave him a glass of water, waited as he kicked off his shoes and settled into the couch, then turned out the lights and went back to my bedroom. A few hours later when I got up, I saw that he was gone— the blanket folded and resting on the arm of the couch.

I spent the rest of the day doing household chores, found an hour or so to write, and soon forgot that Keith had even been around, until Sunday afternoon, when there was another series of rapid knocks at the door.

It was Keith, sober and apologetic with a lopsided smile, asking if he could take me to dinner to make up for his bad behavior.

I told him I had been shopping earlier and had enough food to cook dinner for both us—if he didn't mind burgers.

As I cooked, we chatted about the office, the college town, New York, and Texas, but nothing about Rachel, or Keith's behavior the night before. Keith was a coworker and higher up in the company hierarchy, so I understood that there were boundaries in place we should try to avoid crossing. The subject surfaced as we were eating—Keith explained that they were divorcing and splitting up. He didn't appear ashamed or disturbed, and his explanation for the separation was a calmly noted "we both saw it coming." Rachel would stay in the rental house they had now. Keith said that he had found an apartment in a house in the next town and could move in at the middle of the month. Until then he was staying at Greg's house.

"That must be miserable," I said with a lighthearted laugh. "Colleen must go around plumping up the pillows behind you."

His laughter was refreshing, and put us both at ease. After he helped me clean up the dishes, we sat and watched a video I had rented—a comedy about a couple kidnapping a child. At the end, as he was digging into his pants pockets for his car keys, I mentioned that he could stay here, on the couch, if he didn't want to impose on Greg and Colleen. I felt certain that he would not cross this boundary.

But he liked the idea. "You wouldn't mind?" he asked.

My gesture was sincere. I liked Keith and wanted to think of him as a friend. "We could rearrange some of the furniture to give you more privacy," I said, perhaps with too much animation and delight. There was a small room off to the side and I mentioned we could move the couch in there.

"We could do that another time," he said. "This will work for tonight."


I was conscious of his presence in the other room. I heard the television go off. I saw the light go out.

I heard the springs in the couch sag against his weight and the tugging at the blanket as it slipped around his body.

The first time I slept with Eric in college, lying in my bed in the room we shared in our fraternity house, I silently willed him to make the first move, thinking that if I sent out the mental vibes that I might be gay and wanted to know what sex was like with another guy, maybe we might try it out together. It didn't work the first time I did it, nor the second or the third, but at some point, all the energy and vibes coalesced and one night Eric slipped out of his bed and into mine. It wasn't romantic, and it unleashed many other confusions. I was so lost in thoughts of Eric that I did not hear Keith rise off the couch and walk through the cottage, but I finally noticed his dim silhouette in the door frame.

"Everything okay?" I asked. I could see the outline of his boxers and the large T-shirt I had given him to sleep in.

"Just thinking," he answered. "Can't fall asleep."

"You can stay in here if you want," I said. "It might be more comfortable than the couch."

I had brought my bed from my Manhattan apartment, the first and only real piece of furniture I owned, acquired the year I arrived in New York. I had found it in a store in Soho and it had been delivered to my apartment in the West Village in a box full of pieces, the instructions in sketches and Danish. It had been a part of the excitement of landing in a new place, assembling the frame that would be a part of a new life.

Keith slipped into the bed and lay on his back, looking up at the ceiling. I turned on my side so that I was facing him, watching his chest rise and fall, till he rolled over and faced me.

"Okay?" I whispered.

He nodded and I moved in closer so that he could press his head against my neck and my arm fell around him and landed against his back. We stayed like that for what seemed like a long time, breathing, embracing. I wasn't offering him sex, only comfort. He moved his hand where it had been placed against the blanket, so that it reached my bare waist, then slipped it up beneath my T-shirt so it landed against my chest. He lifted his face up and we slipped into a kiss, the pressure of his stubble against my own waking me.

I wasn't going to press for more, breaking away from the kiss, but his hand was now against my chest, so I turned and slipped my arms around him and beneath his shirt.

I was trying to go at whatever speed he was willing, not attempting to pounce or take advantage of him. If kissing and fondling were all we were going to do, I would be fine and as grateful for it as I hoped he would be. But when his hand drifted below my waist, I knew that the boundaries had been cleared. There was little sleep that night for either of us.

This is not a story about Keith, though I count Keith as one of my favorite lovers, and I don't mean that in an entirely sexual manner; the two weeks he stayed with me remains one of my happiest memories. It wasn't a spontaneous relationship of touching and kissing at every moment; it was being companions as adults, a quiet sharing, caring, conversations and laughter, something that I had never really experienced before, even when I was in love with Eric or when I was tending to Mitch.

We kept our confidences confined to our private time together at the cottage—nothing personal between us was carried into the office— we commuted in separate cars; Keith left early and arrived back at the cottage late. Greg and Alan and Colleen were all unsuspecting—aware only that Keith was separating from his wife and staying with a friend "from his gym." All of this seemed to have escaped Maggie's attention too; her mood darkened every day. She tossed her hair, tilted her head, and scribbled furiously in her journal. She had not told her team of architects that she was pregnant, and I was confused why she was keeping it a secret, though I knew it was no more a secret in the office than my affair with Keith.

I made space for Keith's clothes and other belongings in the small room where I kept a bookcase and my bike. It wasn't an amicable breakup. Rachel was angry and stubborn; she called the cottage in the evenings and Keith would lean against the wall, then slide to the floor and try to end the argument. There was a continued debate on whether she would stay or return to Texas, where her family was. Her hesitancy to leave revolved around Keith. She wanted a long separation before filing for divorce.

I understood that Keith had placed himself in exile—transitioning from a married life to a single one, and maybe from identifying as straight to gay—and my purpose was mostly a functional one, to aid with this transition. He was upset over Rachel, missed her, concerned that he was hurting her, that he had made a mistake of her life. He spoke of wanting something new—leaving the brand-name architect and his firm to work elsewhere, doing something other than executing blueprints, starting over. I was as supportive as I could figure out how to be; I was aware that our relationship was going to be a limited one, that perhaps when

Keith landed on his feet elsewhere, I might be the collateral damage. There was no talk about a theoretical "us" together in the future. I was happy to share my time and home with him as a friend would; of course, I wanted more, but this was not my sole decision to make.

Our most intimate conversations happened in bed, in the dark, when the day was almost over and we were close to falling asleep. One evening Keith talked a long while about his older brother and his mother's determination to keep him alive. My recollections of Mitch and Wade and Peter and Adrian and Stuart took shapes and meanings. It felt easy to articulate their shortcomings to Keith—he was a friend first. "We" were not reality, only an unspoken "temporary intimacy." Stuart called one evening and when I told him that I couldn't speak to him because I had a friend over, he hung up and I never heard from him again. Jesse was annoyed when I mentioned I had a "houseguest."

"Is this a private club?" he asked, "Or are you selling memberships?"

"It's complicated," I answered.

"Isn't everything?"

My concerns and feelings weren't the important ones. I couldn't have handled this if it had happened a year before; my own psychic turmoil would have left me needy and defensive. Because I had also placed myself in exile when I left Manhattan, I had learned that time and distance had a way of offering a method to heal yourself. Did I love Keith? Yes, I loved him immediately, in a way I hadn't felt with anyone before, but I didn't tell him this because I held myself back. To do so would have been to take advantage of him when he was at a low point.

We loaded up a rental van the day Keith moved into his new apartment. Rachel was absent when we carried out boxes and bags from their rented house. We drove to a thrift shop on the highway and found a bed frame and a new mattress from a discount store. I knew that our relationship—or bond—was ending. There was no offer from Keith for me to stay the night at his new place and I didn't press a desire to be there. I felt my own need began to surface. In a way I am grateful that he understood this.

But the uneasiness I felt at work was not from being around Keith. Something with Maggie was unraveling. She had grown more quiet. And she sat at her desk and cried and then locked herself into the bathroom. One day I walked down the crazy flights of stairs and found Colleen and asked her to talk to Maggie because something was not right. She gave me a stern look and said, "It's best to stay away from things that don't concern you."

It was an odd statement, which I didn't understand until I found a moment to ask Alan. "She hasn't said anything to me," he answered. "And I'm not supposed to gossip. I believe her husband sent his son to a boarding school."

I was lucky the weather had warmed and I was able to take up biking again, and I believe that being in motion and staying alone and introspective helped keep my emotions clear and navigable. I knew that I had changed as well in the time I had spent with Keith, and I took trips to bike in parks further west, the plants and flowers just beginning to awaken, and then, a few weeks later, I returned to New York for a weekend visit, inserting myself into Jesse's chaotic life.

The trip to New York was a therapeutic one; I was aware of how much my life in New York had shaped me and was still a part of who I was. I wasn't there as a tourist. And I wasn't there as a visitor. I was someone who had awakened from a long dream, someone returning to his hometown where everything had changed. Jesse seemed less agile, as if his anger had seeped into his bones and created needles of pain as he moved. He had gotten tickets to an off-off-Broadway showcase which he squirmed through. Afterward, we ate at a restaurant in the Village with one of the cast members and his boyfriend. It made me envious and wistful of the life I had left behind in Manhattan, though Jesse only pushed his food from one side of his plate to another. He had a growing concern about his editing job at the mathematics journal—there were now limited sick days, higher insurance co-pays; he wanted to leave but couldn't continue without the health coverage. When I asked about the status of his book, he brightened, since the focus was directed at him, though he rambled into a bitter rant of an in-house lawyer wanting to tone down his accusations against named government and religious officials.

Walking slowly to the subway later, Jesse mentioned that an apartment in his building was coming up for rent soon and did I want to see about it? "It's across the hall from me," he said. "It'll make it so much easier for you to take out my trash."

I realized, then, that this was Jesse reaching out. And I understood that he was now my responsibility, my path, my decision, my next move. I told him to keep me updated about the apartment. A cold gust of wind clutched me by the throat and shook the sense back into me. Did I love being in the city more than I loved being away from it? Or had I just needed to experience one to understand the other? Perhaps my mistakes were a deeper bend of my learning curve.

Spring arrived, and the heat rose up the stairs. Maggie grew fragile and called in sick frequently. She seldom talked to me and what I learned about her, I heard from others. She and Bryan had separated and she was now living at her mother's house.

Keith took trips to Los Angeles to oversee some construction issues. I did not hear from him for days. I knew that this was a pattern he was trying to set. When he returned, he was aloof and quiet. We'd only been sexually intimate twice since he had moved out, the first time to remember, the last as if to forget.

I heard it first from Greg, which was why it angered me.

"We need to send drafts to L.A. this evening," Greg said, leaning over my shoulder. "I need to be home with my daughter for a few hours so Keith will bring them to you."

I sensed him stretching up, backing away, as if he held some unsaid secret, so I swiveled my stool around to look at him for any last-minute instructions. "Next Friday, the team's planning something for Keith's last day. I'm sure he'd want you to come too."

He gave me that lopsided grin, as if he knew he was messing with my head. He backed up further, turned and hurried down the small flight of stairs.

I grew flushed. I felt my confusion rise, but I didn't have a chance to respond because Alan was coming up the steps that Greg had just cleared.

"Can you cover the museum team today? Maggie is out."

"Just today?"

He stopped and looked at me. He knew I knew more about her whereabouts than he did.

"I don't know."

"Keith's leaving?" I asked him, just as he turned away again.

He gave me another slow look, as if he didn't want to discuss it with me.

"Why does everyone know this except me?"

"I can't answer that," he said, a tinge of sympathy in his voice. "You know that."

I could tell from his expression that he knew about us too, or had heard some gossip about it, and I felt my eyes welling up.

"Did he say why?" I asked.

"He's gotten another opportunity," Alan answered. "With a firm in L.A."

"L.A.?"

Alan didn't respond and, to check my confusion and depression, I pressed him about another subject. "Can something be done about the heat up here?"

"We have someone working on it."

"What does that mean?"

"It means that I'll discuss it with Ian at some point."

"At some point? I've been complaining about this for over a year."

He didn't have anything else to say to me and left with an exasperated look on his face. I was hurt that Keith had not confided in me about his decision to move to Los Angeles. The museum team began bringing memos and drawings. I stuffed them into tubes, broke into a sweat, and rinsed my face at the sink in the small bathroom, revisiting conversations with Keith in my mind over and over. At lunchtime I left the building and biked to a park and ate the sandwich and an apple I had brought with me that morning. I started and stopped myself from crying, convincing myself that I would not let this be a setback.

When I returned to my desk the museum team had left more drawings and memos for me to prepare for L.A. But it was the temperature of the workspace that crushed me. Or changed me. My mission seemed suddenly clear. I calmly walked down the stairs to the ground floor. I knew the famous architect was in the office that day. I'd seen his expensive brand-name car in the parking lot when I came back from lunch. His assistant Debby was still out to lunch and the door to his office was open. I took a few cautious steps, saw his wave of white hair and a reflection of light from his large eyeglasses. He was reading at his desk, so I tapped on his door and entered the room.

I introduced myself and told him I worked in the small space at the top of the building, under the eaves of the roof. He gave me a look as if he might have seen me before, coming and going from the building, nodded, but didn't say anything to indicate I should leave or stay.

"At this moment, the temperature in that workspace is close to 100 degrees and there is no air circulation, no window or ventilation system in place. I have photos and items that document this—not just today, but over the course of the year that I have worked here. A year in which I doubt that you have even bothered to learn my name. But that's immaterial to me. I don't care about that. I do care about my working conditions. If something is not done within the next hour to alleviate the excessive heat that I have been subjected to during the time frame of my employment here, I am calling the fire department, the police department, the State Department of Labor, and the Department of Health to file complaints. I will hire an attorney to prosecute you and the firm for not only allowing harmful work conditions but for designing and approving them as well. And I will call *The New*

*York Times,* the *Philadelphia Inquirer* and anyone I can get to answer the phone at *Architectural Digest* and begin to tell the story of how you are incapable of designing your own office space to comply with acceptable work standards."

I knew that I had included a lot of frivolous facts as insults in my demented tirade, but I didn't wait for a response from him. I turned and walked out of his office, my heart thudding in my chest so fiercely that I was worried I would not make it back up the stairs. But I did make it back to the overheated boomerang and I took a breath of the hot air and began to attach signed memos to the blueprints and roll them into tubes as sweat began to dribble beneath my armpits.

Ten minutes later, Alan, with Ian, the chief operating officer, appeared at my desk, red-faced and angry. "Why didn't you come to me first?" he asked.

"I did. A year ago."

I was hoping I would be fired and I could walk away in a proud, dramatic show of defiance, and I could go on unemployment and welfare and food stamps and live a happy life in poverty. And I hoped that Ian's job was on the line. And Alan's and Greg's. I was ready to take the whole building down and the firm and the brand-name idiot architect along with it.

"We're setting up a temporary space at the top of the stairs where you can work today. You'll have to make do with just a typewriter and use the photocopier here. We'll have a new space set up for you tomorrow. We're meeting later today about where to locate you."

An hour later, after enduring the annoyed looks of the exasperated staff who wandered in and out of the overheated workspace helping to carry my desk items down the small flight of stairs, I was sitting at the top platform of the stairs behind a short trophy case that had lost its three-dimensional architectural model and now supported the weight of an electric typewriter. I felt humiliated, as if I had been ordered to sit in a corner with a dunce cap on my head. But it was considerably cooler than the attic space and as I got used to the holding the typewriter in place as I pecked at the keys, I was able to finish typing and copying memos and get the packages downstairs in time for the mail pickup.

Alan had sheepishly appeared and disappeared throughout the process, unapologetic and managerial, but he appeared again as I was shifting around items before I went home for the day. I thought he might have news about where in the building I would be working the following day, or better yet, an offer for me to quietly leave the company without stirring up any further trouble. Instead, he told me that he had heard from Maggie's mother. Maggie was in the hospital. "A miscarriage," he said.

I asked for the details. The room number, the hospital, what complications she was experiencing. He answered my questions, reminding me he was only informing me of the details, "as a friend."

"She doesn't want any visitors," he added.

I nodded. I didn't expect that she would. And I didn't expect that I would visit her, even though at that moment she was deep in my thoughts because I wanted to share the horror of my own day with her.

"I shouldn't tell you this," Alan added, looking around to make sure no one was nearby within earshot. "They took your threat of a lawsuit seriously."

One of Maggie's illogical stanzas went through my mind, suddenly making sense: *fire shall challenge water if water does not challenge land.*

"I meant it seriously," I said.

"You should be careful. They're going to be watching you more closely," he said. "Looking for their own reasons. You understand what I am saying?"

We were interrupted by Keith bolting down the stairs toward me and the temporary workspace. He looked flushed and uneasy and I thought he might be showing up now to tell me of his departure. Instead, he regarded Alan and I noticed him shut down and lock me out. His warmth disappeared and he transformed into another person. His postured stiffened, his eyes grew distant, and his jaw tightened. "Is it too late to add another memo to the package?" he asked me.

"Yes," I answered dryly. "It's too late."


The following day I phoned in sick, hearing Alan's gasp of exasperation before I hung up. I went out for a long bike ride. The heat was bearable, the humidity thick, the green of the landscapes intensive and bright, but I was happy. When I returned to the cottage, I showered and then phoned Jesse in New York. He answered in a good mood—he'd seen a galley of his book, but he was now battling an infection on his foot—"I thought this was supposed to wreak havoc on my internal organs, not my toenails!"

I brought him up to date on the latest events and at the end of listening to my anecdotes he reminded me that there was an empty apartment across the hall in his building. I asked about the cost of the rent, the landlord, and his advice on whether I should return to New York. "We could be like Lucy and Ethel," he said. "The gay version."

Alan was waiting for me when I arrived the next morning at work. My workspace had been set up in the far corner of the L.A. team room, shifting around the draftspersons and junior architects. Keith had been relocated in another team room since he had given his notice and only had a week left before his departure.

Greg was not pleased with the new arrangements. It meant that all of us were now under surveillance and he no longer had an unsupervised opportunity for goading me. What had been a casual work environment for him and his buddies was now a shared space of scrutiny and fear. I knew from the moment I sat at the new desk that I would leave the firm as soon as possible. I knew that my healing time in the college town was at an end. That evening after work I drove to Manhattan, buzzed Jesse's apartment, saw the empty apartment next door, and met with the landlord—a barber who worked in a shop on the ground floor of the building—to sign a lease. I realized it wasn't a hasty decision—I'd been thinking about it all along. I wasn't running away from the college town—there was nothing there to make me stay—I had gone there to find the strength that I had lost, to take apart all the little pieces of myself, give them a good cleaning, and put them back together again. I was returning to live in Manhattan, to begin the life I had left behind. That night I slept on Jesse's couch and left early the next morning to drive to the college town and the office. I worked quietly until lunchtime, then left the building and walked the three blocks to the house where Maggie was staying with her mom.

Maggie answered the door. She was pale, bewildered, and clearly wanted me to go away.

"I wanted you to be the first one to know," I said. "I'm quitting. I'm moving back to New York."

She brightened and hugged me, gathered up her hair with one hand and led me inside.

She was beautiful and ethereal; she tried to keep herself detached and distant and whispery but her cleverness would break through. We sat and talked for about an hour—away from ringing phones, interrupting architects, and the relentless heat and gloom of the office. She wanted to know where in the city the apartment was, what kind of work I would be doing. As I looked at my watch, I laid out another plan to her. I mentioned my tirade to the famous architect and Alan's subsequent remark that they were worried about possible lawsuits. "Did you formally resign?" I asked her.

She shook her hair and placed it against one shoulder and said she was on an undocumented leave of absence. But she doubted that she would return and she didn't expect that they would want her back. "I'm sure your father can suggest an attorney in town," I said, "who could make a claim that the work conditions attributed to your... problems."

She looked down at her hands. "I can't drag anyone else into this," she said.

"The working conditions were not adequate, Maggie. It could have caused damage to your health. At least think about it."

As I stood up to go, she said softly. "You know, don't you?"

"Know what?"

"About Luke."

"He's finishing the year at another school, right?"

She withdrew into herself; her lips went slack and her eyes welled. "Luke was... the baby's father."

I didn't know. Not for certain. Not until Maggie said it. I wanted to ask her why, though I knew the answer already. Maggie was fragile and unstable, Bryan was distant and unavailable, Luke was young and curious. It had crossed my mind a couple of times, particularly the way she often spoke so fondly about her stepson.

I sat down beside her and held her until she had composed herself. Then, I asked her what her plans were.

She looked at me as though I was mad. And this time I knew that I wasn't. Instead, I saw her grief, her depression, her confusion. I didn't know what to say, so I sat and talked to her about losing Mitch. And Wade. And Peter. And Eric. And my worries about Jesse. "It doesn't go away," I said. "So I have to find things to make myself feel better."

Because of my new work location, under Greg's watchful eye, I seldom had time to assist the museum team. I also had to limit my phone calls with Jesse until we could speak more freely when I was at home in the cottage. Keith appeared at my desk only to hand off tasks. His disregard of me was upsetting, but I refused to let it show.

I waited until the last possible moment on Friday to walk down to Alan's office and tell him of my decision. "I wanted to talk to you," he said, as I appeared at his door. "Get your opinion on some things. We were thinking about expanding your role. Giving you more responsibility. A raise. Maggie's not coming back and we thought that maybe you could manage an assistant, take over supervising some of the administrative functions. The firm would pay for any training courses you think would be appropriate."

"I'm afraid I've already signed a lease for a new apartment in New York," I said. "I came down to tell you my last day will be next Friday."

He held in his surprise, but I noticed his eyes grow harder. "You don't have to make such a hasty departure. The firm could get you out of the lease if the landlord gave you any trouble."

"I think you know it's time for me to leave."

He mentioned that the famous brand-name architect would want me to sign a confidentiality agreement.

"He might want that, but an agreement takes two parties to come to terms. Not one."

"There could be a bonus payment included."

"A payoff."

"As a friend, I wish it didn't have to end like this."

"As a friend, I wish it didn't have to end like this, too."


I had been working nearby at a temp job, filing documents for a designer, and after work I walked down Ninth Avenue. It was mid-March, the afternoons still felt short. It was chilly, but there was a hopeful feeling spring could arrive soon. I stopped at the deli and ordered a sandwich and a soda, then rounded the corner and went up the front stairs to

Mitch's apartment building. The day nurse greeted me when I came in the door, saying two friends had just been visiting and left. I placed my sandwich bag on the table, hung up my jacket, and went to the sofa bed where Mitch slept. The nurse followed me, whispering, "you should say your goodbyes now."

I'd been staying evenings in Mitch's apartment for almost two months. Sometimes I would sleep with him on the sofa bed, my arms threaded through the IV lines and around Mitch's waist. Sometimes I slept nearby on the floor, in case he needed help to reach the toilet.

That evening Mitch was lying on his back. His eyes were closed. His breathing was shallow. I didn't want to believe that this might be his last day. There was a knock at the door—it was the evening nurse, and I listened to their whispers as they assessed Mitch's status. The evening nurse—a fellow named Damien who lived in Queens—asked me if there was any need for last rites. Did I need to phone someone?

I had a headache from reading too much at work, the stress that I carried, and the warm temperature inside the apartment. I stood in the kitchen and took a few bites of my sandwich, sipped at the soda, and went back to the chair beside Mitch's bed.

His hands were ice cold. I tried rubbing them to warm them up. I sat there for a few minutes, looking at the IV stand, the tube that ran beneath Mitch's T-shirt, the tumble of blankets around his feet.

Mitch's lips began to move, but there was no sound. He raised his right hand into the air, as if to cup the side of someone's face, and then his left hand began to rise. His feet shifted; his knees bending and rising. He looked as if he was reaching out, waiting to be uplifted to the sky.

His soul left slowly, like rising smoke. His body sank back to the bed and was still. Damien checked for a pulse. A phone call was made to the police and two large men crowded into the apartment. I phoned Mitch's sister. The morticians arrived and zipped his body into a black body bag. I watched them carry his body out into the hall.

I gathered my knapsack and a few other items around the apartment. As Damien and I shut the apartment door, the police sealed it with yellow tape.

These were my last minutes with Mitch. I would replay them in my mind for years. I'd love to believe that Mitch's outstretched arms were a certain sign that there was an afterlife amongst the stars.

I wish I had a better resolution for this story; that Greg confessed his undying love for me, or that Keith convinced me to move with him to Los Angeles. My final day working for the brand-name architect was also Keith's last, and my send-off read only as a footnote to the farewell he was given by the team of would-be famous draftsmen. I had opted out of attending his bon voyage festivities—and when my workday came to an end, no one was to be found—Greg had deserted his desk, Keith had left for the restaurant, and even Alan was not in his office. In many ways I am grateful for this—I am never prepared to say goodbye to anyone, which was one of the reasons why my life in New York had become so dispiriting. I left the renovated shell of an office, walked along the corridor of trophy shelves and three-dimensional models for the last time, and got on my bike, the warm air blowing on my arms as I cycled to the cottage.

I have left out many things that happened to me during my time living in the college town because they would only be distractions in an already complicated narrative. I haven't included the day that Maggie played the piano for me and the amazement and pride I felt at witnessing her talent. I haven't written about my foolish attempt to plant wildflowers outside the cottage, which resulted only in weeds and the complaint of the property manager, nor of my failed attempt to build a doghouse in hopes of adopting a pet from the nearby animal shelter. I haven't included the owners of the large estate or details of the lunches I suffered through in an effort to fit in to their specifications. I never had an opportunity to know Dan better, the bike shop owner and instructor, but I don't count that as one of my regrets. I haven't mentioned the portraits I drew with the colored pencils I stole from the architects' desks in attempts to shift my mind away from a staggering depression. I don't think I included enough about how hard it was to stop smoking, nor do I believe I have given enough weight to the fear and anxiety that after every sexual encounter there was always the question mark of testing HIV-positive.

I delivered a set of groceries and knickknacks to the elderly couple at the farmhouse and said goodbye, explaining to them that I was moving on. I could see the disappointment and worry in their smiles, the same expressions I had witnessed in my parents years ago when I left for Manhattan.

The movers arrived at the cottage and I was headed back to New York City with a new car, a secondhand bicycle, and a well-worn bed. The car would last a year until I sold it to a friend. The bike would last longer; I would carry it on my shoulder down five flights of stairs and walk it to Central

Park, where I would cycle the laps with other adventurous urban dwellers. Eventually I would hoist it onto a treadmill during the winter months and then abandon it for Rollerblades. But the joy it provided has always remained with me because of the therapy and healing power of its motion.

The famous architect and his business team tried further scare tactics even after I returned to live in Manhattan—threatening to withhold my final salary paycheck and earned vacation payments unless I signed a confidentiality agreement, and finally, attempting to bill me for long distance phone charges, all of which I successfully batted away.

Life in New York returned with all of its complications. I was once again rock-bottom poor. AIDS had not disappeared from the landscape; in fact, it continued with a fury. More friends would die, more disappointments would arrive, depression would return and then abate.

Jesse's book was a great success. And gave his acid tongue a notoriety that extended around the globe. He never stopped being an AIDS activist. He adored the attention. He did interviews with anyone who asked and could be counted on to mouth sharp remarks on any topic, but mostly he talked about himself. He wrote two more novels. The mathematics journal was kind to him, granting him extended leaves and allowing him to maintain his health insurance.

I volunteered writing for an AIDS magazine, profiles of men and women dealing with HIV issues. Taking care of Mitch made me a better man. Mitch made me able to take care of Jesse. My evolution as a gay man continued. My expectations changed when I realized I was not as honest and truthful and trusting as I wanted another man to be. I found lovers but no partners. Jesse remained my best friend and became the family I needed, until he, too, left me. He was thirty-nine when he died. It was another devastating loss.

I wrote a book, and then another. A novel. Short stories. Essays and reviews, proving, I hope, that there is a future for all college English majors if this is the path they should seek, and publication can be achieved without a mentor or a graduate degree from a writing program. It all looks impressive on my resume, if not in my bank account.

It's taken me many years to write about this particular episode of my life. I believe that's because for a long time I only focused on the details of it over and over, much like a war veteran recounts horrific battles and the loss of his buddies. My story of these years is only one of many. It seems appropriate now to mention that Maggie was not a survivor. Her spiral downward was quick. Her overdose planned.

So as much as my story is one of my healing, about finding self-worth and redirecting ambition, it's also one infused with pain. And guilt. And regret.

I fear I may have also overplayed the importance of astrology to this story and given more heft to the deliberations of Tarot cards, though its uncertain interpretations remind me of Maggie and her unexpected gifts of friendship and wisdom, and then about the would-be architect and what becomes more and more oddly the memory of an idyllic exile from the city. If there is anything I learned from being born on the same day as Oscar Wilde, it is that life doesn't always happen the way you wish it might be.

One day a few years after I had resettled in Manhattan, as a snowstorm was moving into the city, I stood in front of my fifth-story apartment window watching the snow fall along Ninth Avenue, bringing the traffic below to a halt. My phone rang and when I answered it, I heard Keith's voice breaking through the static of the connection. He was calling from Los Angeles, where it was warm and sunny.

We talked a moment about the weather—perhaps to ease my shock and curiosity at his call. I thought perhaps he was arranging a trip to the city and wanted to meet for dinner or drinks and recall former times. But then he said, "I realize I didn't tell you this long ago. It was too difficult at the time. The timing wasn't right."

My gaze drifted to the window and I felt time slowing down, the falling snow paused by a breath of air. "I loved you," Keith said. "I wish I had been able to tell you that."

My first concern, of course, was that something was wrong, that his admission was fueled by regret, and his guilt was due to his being ill or having had some kind of setback. He assured me all was fine, but it was in that assurance that I sensed all was not as he described it to be. Even if he wasn't ill, I knew he was calling to say goodbye, the goodbye we'd never had years before and which he now needed to make in order to proceed to the next chapter of his life. We talked for about an hour, the light dimming, the snow glowing as the blue-white hues settled on the roofs and window ledges. It was a wistful, sentimental conversation, something only time and distance would allow.

# Acknowledgments

I am indebted to the editors who acquired and/or edited many of my early short stories and essays that were used as a touchstone to create this work, and to my fellow writers and readers for their encouragement to continue to tell stories about the impact of AIDS. I am thankful to Kevin Bentley for his insightful edits of my books and writings, including my first draft of this story. And I am grateful to Jay Blotcher for his enthusiasm and expertise in guiding me toward the completion of the final manuscript of this novel.

## About the Author

Jameson Currier is the author of eight novels, five collections of short fiction, three illustrated tales, and a memoir. His short fiction has appeared in many literary magazines, anthologies, and Web sites. His AIDS-themed short stories were translated into French by Anne-Laure Hubert and published as *Les Fantômes*. His novel, *The Third Buddha*, about the aftermath of 9/11 in Manhattan and Afghanistan, was translated into French by Étienne Gomez and published as *Le Troisième Bouddha* by Perspective cavalière and was awarded the Prix du Roman Gay. His reviews, essays, interviews, and articles on AIDS and gay culture have been published in many national and local publications. He also wrote the documentary film: *Living Proof: HIV and the Pursuit of Happiness.* In 2010, he founded Chelsea Station Editions, an independent press devoted to gay literature. The press serves as the home for Mr. Currier's own writings which now span a career of more than five decades. Books published by the press have been honored by the Lambda Literary Foundation, the American Library Association GLBTRT Roundtable, the Saints and Sinners Literary Festival, the Gaylactic Spectrum Awards Foundation, the Publishing Triangle, and the Rainbow Book Awards. In 2011, Mr. Currier launched the literary magazine *Chelsea Station*, and in 2014 relaunched the magazine as an online literary site. A self-taught artist, illustrator, and graphic designer, Mr. Currier's design work is tagged as "Peachboy" and his original art is signed "Jimmy." In 2020, he established Chatham Junction Studio, which serves as the curator for his expanding body of original art. Mr. Currier has been a member of the Board of Directors of the Arch and Bruce Brown Foundation, a recipient of a fellowship from New York Foundation for the Arts, and a judge for many literary competitions. He currently divides his time between a studio apartment in New York City and a farmless farmhouse in the Hudson Valley.

www.ingramcontent.com/pod-product-compliance
Lightning Source LLC
Chambersburg PA
CBHW030333030726
47499CB00003B/750